Driving Backwards

An inspirational story of hope and healing

Carol A Peterson,
carol.drivingbackwards@gmail.com

Good Piper Studio

It is with a grateful heart that I dedicate this book
to my husband Bob, whom God brought into
my life, after my late husband died.
Bob is an engineer by trade,
which means numbers, formulas, and
mathematical principles govern his thinking.
He is not touchy-feely.
Yet, with enthusiasm, he proofed my
manuscript many times.
He even teared up once or twice.
His insights and suggestions
improved my story.
Working with him proved joyful and
endearing as we brought my book to print.
Let's do this again soon, my love.

Thank you to Shawna Wakefield for being my first reader and giving me an honest review. I used your suggestion. **Yes, there will be a sequel.**

Tracey Rene' Williams Bisconer, you of the eagle eye. Thank you for catching more whoopsee's and helping my second printing read better.

<u>Reviews</u>

Driving Backwards is a "good read" with enough mild adventure and "what's going to happen next" story to keep you turning the page to see where this will take Janine and you. It sends a message of patience, fortitude, and positivity to anyone going through any of life's challenges.
Maxine EMc Osborne

"I am reading your book [Driving Backwards]. It brought me to tears. The story and the way you wrote it   with so much incredible descriptions is truly amazing and I read books all the time." Ingrid T.

"I don't even want to finish the book cuz I don't want it to end." Sara
"I loved Driving Backwards so much that I had to read it twice. Quite a story; believable and sincere. I loved meeting Harley. The Harley's in my life were a beacon in my storm." Tracey WB

To My Readers

I have walked alongside of grieving friends
and have faced loss as well.
I felt it was an important issue to address
as a novel instead of a "how to" book.
Grief is profoundly personal and every person deals
with sorrow in their own way and in their own timing.
If you are now or have ever faced grief,
I hope this story brings a measure
of comfort and healing to you.

Sincerely,
Carol
carol.drivingbackwards@gmail.com

Preface

How this story came to be.

I started writing this book years ago. After I had a few chapters done, I emailed it to a writer friend for her input. She returned it, calling it "unreadable." I stopped writing. Yet, this story wouldn't leave me alone. I picked up my pen [computer] and wrote and wrote, for the sheer pleasure of writing, developing my characters and learning where they would take me.

In the Fall of 2024, I realized I had almost finished crafting my story. Oh, my gosh!! Now what? I started educating myself about cover design, editing programs, publishing, and marketing.

When my manuscript was done, I went on through the editing process. Writing is immensely rewarding. Editing is a long and tedious work of love [torture], even with outside help. Each new reading brought more corrections. I imagine you'll stumble across a few ooops. That's all on me.

Errors aside, I hope this story touches you, and speaks to your heart. May God bless you and keep you.

Carol

carol.drivingbackwards@gmail.com

CHAPTER ONE

This is Me

In less than two months, I will be 29. Not that my age matters. I thought you might want to know a bit about me since I am ready to reveal a few dark truths. Well, it's more like I'm trying to walk out of a very dark and shattered place, and I would like some company. I am beginning to question if the present will be my future. Am I locked into my past? Or, does hope still resound within me, strong enough to pull me out if this darkness.

Besides being almost 29, I'm a physical therapist; a career where the seeds were planted when I was twelve. I have always been a planner, and I locked on to PT when my little brother Danny, at the ripe old age of eight, crashed his bike playing road racer. He messed up his foot and ankle badly, which required PT; I became his masseuse and drill sergeant. I flexed his foot gently, rubbed his ankle and calf, then stretched the foot a little further each day. I became totally absorbed when pushing him through the daily drills, um exercises. After seven months, he could run without pain, ride his bike and climb trees. He was a kid once again. I had helped my brother heal; he regained the full use of his foot and ankle. I did that with my very own hands. I was hooked and knew right then that I wanted to grow up to be a physical therapist, and I did.

My chosen career fits my personality too. As a girl who loved the outdoors. I preferred being at the top of a tree rather than playing with dolls. I naturally gravitated towards sports. Any sport. All sports. I was an athlete and built like one. From my early high school days, I was 5'10" with no curves; well, the minimum required. I got my height from Dad's side of the family. It came with long, sturdy legs, toned muscles and good posture, which took discipline during those years when I was the tallest kid in my class. My blonde unruly hair was short and efficient, which made it easier to be outside playing; no need to style the mop that longer hair would have demanded. My attire was no fuss, jeans and t-shirts, and my attitude was win, win, win. Even if I didn't win, I enjoyed every moment trying to win.

My dad, at 6'3" was the mayor of Langley, on Whidbey Island where I grew up. Don't think politicians. Think small town, good guy, gregarious, everyone's friend and always willing to lend a helping hand to whoever needed it. My younger brother Danny grew up to be much like my dad and chose ministry as his way of giving back and helping others. He's an Anglican priest. They are the priests that can marry. You can imagine how happy mom was about the marrying part. Grandbabies!

Mom, a petite 5'4" accountant was the solid foundation of our very outgoing family, strict about two aspects of life; everyone eats dinner together and we go to church on Sundays. Totally opposite of her number-crunching workweek persona, she was also the instigator of some of our greatest adventures. Petite, gentle but a total risk taker when it came to trying new things or exploring the path less taken.

Danny, my younger brother, fell between our parents at 5'8". Yup, I was the big sister in every way.

That's me and my family in a nutshell. Who would have thought we would have faced a tragedy that took me out completely? It is only now, almost a year afterwards, that I can face what happened. My family felt powerless after multiple attempts to come alongside me, even in their own distress.

When tragedy struck my life, I did not respond the way I had always thought I would. To respond would have taken some kind of self-determined action, to plan, to push through it. You know all those motivational sport's sayings I lived with and spoke regularly. Nope, didn't happen. In truth, I took no action, I became incapable of planning. All my life, action was an adjective often used when people thought of me. Tragedy vanquished that part of me. It swallowed me up, then gnawed at the very core of who I was. One devastating loss was compounded by another and another until I curled up like a pill-bug in a thunderstorm, that hard shell became the last vestige of self-protection against the cruelties raining down on me.

I left my daughter Casey's grave, my husband's bed, my PT job just as a partnership was about to be offered, and I walked away from our Whidbey Island home and my family. On autopilot, I sold my car, hopped on a plane, and headed south. I took refuge in the guest room of my Aunt Sally's home in Mesa, Arizona. Besides a duffle bag of clothes, the only accompaniment I had was my little dog, Peaches. Even though I shipped my bike separately, I never rode it.

My parents fled as well. After months of trying to save me from myself, all the while bearing their own grief, my parents did something they had only alluded to in the past. They retired. They found they needed to rebuild their own broken, hurting lives. A glimmer of my mother's sense of adventure surfaced. They bought a motorhome to travel. Or were they, too, running away in a nicely decked-out home on wheels?

Loss does that. It threw us in a pit and made each of us reevaluate life or hide from reality. For my parents, that meant running in a sane manner, living out one of their dreams and hopefully in doing so, bringing comfort to their broken hearts. They had lost their granddaughter and no matter what they tried, they couldn't break through to me, their only daughter. It became essential to heal themselves.

I was unreachable. Anytime someone tried to come close, to reach out, to soothe, or to share in my grief, I withdrew further. Like that pill-bug, I pulled that shell around me even tighter. I repelled any attempts at solace by hiding in my protective casing, my thick, impenetrable armor. Month after month, I was barely living as I hid within that unbreakable sheath.

CHAPTER TWO

Reverse

A few months ago, softly, life whispered its first call into my heart. It was a mere faint sigh which began my awakening. Tragedy is greedy. It reaches out its long arms, sweeping wide and far claiming as many as it can possibly crush within its grip. My whole family, now spread all around the country, was caught in its grasp. I didn't want to be its victim any longer. At an unconscious level, I didn't want this for my family either. Something flickered within me, a faint spark began to take hold. I heard the whisper and yearned to try to leave my darkness and venture out. I felt the need to answer that deep inner cry to crawl out of the gloomy shadows that tried to suck every ounce of life out of me.

I don't want to tell my parents or to drag them into this and add to their distress. I'm afraid. What if I fail? So, I am turning to you. This is where you and I begin. I would like your help. With you, hopefully coming along of me, to give me the courage that is crucial for me to move from my darkness into the light, a glimmer even, of life. Someone to vent to; share my fears.

It's May. The Arizona days were already chattering about who would be the first to hit 100 degrees. I learned my lesson. I hadn't heard the hot-voices yesterday and attempted a long bike ride. That morning, I hit the garage door opener. As it climbed upward; I put on my bright orange bike helmet that coordinated well with today's bright orange and pink biking shirt. I love bright colors and don't even own something in black. Black attire is a definite death wish in AZ; think rapid absorption of unrelenting heat.

This heat was revealed to me as the garage door quietly rose to a bright sunny day. Similar to black attire being a death wish. As is vigorous exercise, once the sun has fully risen. Being focused on the ride ahead and making sure I had all my gear, I was oblivious to the heat. I hopped on my bike and headed out like it was a normal day with the sun warming my back. It quickly turned into the sun chasing me with a blow torches, screaming and ranting words of a maniac killer. It felt like the rubber grips on my handles would soon melt and my hands along with it. H. O. T.

I turned around and peddled home like a possessed person, afraid my tires were melting too. In the shelter of the garage I took my gear off, put the biked on the wall bracket and I sucked in a deep breath of air that was not fire, thinking how glad I was Aunt Sally hadn't witnessed my misadventure.

Back four to five weeks ago when I had emerged from my protective shell, each day brought a greater desire to get my life back, whatever that would look like. With a newfound resolve came introspection; first I had to face what I had hidden from while curled up in Aunt Sally's guest room; to look straight into the abysmal heartbreak that had brought me such anguish. I felt compelled to go back to where it all began; Dungeness Spit on the Olympic Peninsula in Washington.

This desire to go to Dungeness came about by accident or by God's design. The first step was when I felt strong enough to venture out of my aunt's gated community. Long walks had progressed into bike riding and then going for short drives. It was cool enough in April to be outside. You wouldn't believe what happened one day.

I had borrowed my aunt's second vehicle; a beaten and battered old pickup used for hauling whatever needed hauling. After coaxing the truck out of the driveway, I meandered around Mesa, usually getting lost, but trusting my sense of direction to find my way home. Some of my old self, the daring gene, came to life. Thanks mom. My pride on these drives; no GPS for this gal!

I wound around a side street, took a few turns and found myself at a dead end. I stopped and tried to get my bearings. That's when I noticed a camper van with a for-sale sign that sat in a nearly empty apartment parking lot. After peering in a few windows, I impulsively jotted down the number from the for-sale sign on the windshield. It took me a good ten minutes to find my way out of the multiple dead-end streets and locate the road that led back to Aunt Sally's place.

A few nights later, I was wearing my favorite plaid shirt. It was loose and long and well worn. I reached into my pocket and came out with the forgotten slip of paper with the phone number for that van written on it. With fingers moving faster than my hesitant heart could beat, I dialed the number. Two days later, I was the stunned owner of a camper van, much to the curious reaction of my Aunt Sally and myself. What had I done!

Before I go on with my story, let me enlighten you a little about Aunt Sally. I know I sound scattered. Nerves? Bear with me. Once I'm on the road, I'm sure I'll be better. Well, I hope so for your sake.

Ok, Aunt Sally. While my mom had been the epitome of professionalism all my life, Aunt Sally was the artist. She painted, threw pottery, made sculptures out of any materials handy, and designed elaborate fiber art. By doing so, she had become a household name in many of the Arizona communities. She had spent much of each weekend throughout the year traveling within a three-state radius, from one street fair to the next, selling what she had created. My Uncle Drake was the master hauler and set-ter-upper, when his schedule allowed. She had a following and was now retired, living in Mesa, where she taught classes through the junior college and the various parks and rec departments. Those who knew and loved her work had become steady visitors to her website. This worked out really well because they were placing orders. Aunt Sally gave up the extensive traveling she had done before retiring. Uncle Drake embraced the slower pace as well. It gave them time to develop other interests. When questioned if she was truly being retired, Aunt Sally, always joyfully responded, "I'm at home, my days are my own and I get to do what I love."

Uncle Drake passed away five years ago. Crushed by my sweet daughter Casey's death, I had desperately sought Aunt Sally's as a haven with a person well acquainted with death. I also told myself that maybe being creative would be good for me. Instead, I barely left the guest room in Aunt Sally's home, even to eat. There was no reason to leave the room, to be alive, to be creative.

As you know, I recently emerged, though a bit dazed, from my self-imposed solitary confinement. Somewhere from within, life was summoning me. I felt like a fluttering unborn bird, just breaking out of my eggshell, peering over the edge of my safety-nest and seeing this vastness. Could I fly? Could I throw myself into the vibrancy that beckoned from outside the nest? The wings of my heart trembled with both trepidation and a tinge of eagerness.

Little by little, that inner instinct gently urged me forward. After a few days of normal daily routines, getting up, showering, dressing and eating, I ventured out of the gated community that encompassed my aunt's home. Who knew that starting life over again meant getting lost and hitting a dead end? That embracing life would come in the shape of a camper van. I still couldn't believe it. I owned a camper van.

I learn from my mistakes; mostly. The first lesson was not to ride my bike mid-morning, starting in May. My second lesson, which I was about to learn, would be how to approach the raging furnace called morning in Arizona. Still uneducated, I got up, leisurely enjoyed some coffee, let Peaches out in the enclosed backyard for a piddle. I wasn't in any rush. I had a simple goal, to check out the storage capacity in the van and come up with a plan to pack. I went into the garage, pushed the button and headed to the garage door as it was opening. I didn't even need to go out on my bike. BLASTED.

Standing in the garage, hot, hot air from the flames of hell sucked the oxygen out of my lungs. I gasped, step backwards quickly and tried to breathe. Cautiously, I approached the outside, only to be hit again. BLAST. I stepped back inside the garage as the door to the house opened. Aunt Sally stuck her head out.

"Janine dear, this is Mesa in mid-May. It's already ninety one degrees and headed up to over one hundred. Once the sun's been up, like now, breathing is not an option. I suggest you wait until around 7:00 tonight when the sun is going down. It will still be hot, but bearable."

I abandoned my plan.

CHAPTER THREE

On to Another

PLAN

That evening, I scouted out the van's interior. I ran a heavy-duty extension cord into the garage to plug in the refrigerator, hoping it would be cool enough for food in the morning. The next day, way before sun-up, having had no coffee, I loaded up the van. My little helper, Peaches, a 6-pound Yorkie, was underfoot at every step.

Oh, I forgot to tell you about Peaches. She's a love. She has been with me through all of this. Even when the comfort of my sweet companion couldn't penetrate the pain that had shut me down, she stayed by my side. The minute I came back to life, Peaches was right there, eager to take part.

I had brought very few possessions with me, but my parents had dropped off a few boxes when they stopped by. There was enough to decide what items I would take and what I would leave behind. In between trips in and out of the house to load the van or to place a few items to be stored in the garage, I would answer Aunt Sally's probing questions.

I did not fully understand my own motives. I just knew that I had to find my life. Something was pushing me to stop hiding, to crawl out of my self-made exile and to see what lived on the other side of the darkness. I knew my answers to Aunt Sally's inquiries were not fully satisfying, yet I trusted my aunt would accept what I was attempting to do.

During the days of preparation, I was thankful Aunt Sally could not reach my parents, who were traveling while staying "off the grid." As my father would say, "we're exploring places without freeways, highways, or mega malls." That would have been at my mom's urging to take the roads less-traveled.

Off-the-grid also meant that cell phone coverage was spotty. Because of this, I could sort and pack with a lighter heart, not having to answer the barrage of questions, spoken and unspoken, that I knew would come from my parents. I loved them dearly, but right now I needed all my inner stamina to step out into my undefined life.

All too often, their love seemed to dribble over the protective shell I wore. Like wax dribbling down the side of a burning candle, the drippings of their love seemed to smother me, to threaten to extinguish any flame. At some level, I knew this was more about me than my parents' love for me, but mostly I just wanted them to give me space.

CHAPTER FOUR

Tweety-Bird

I had walked out onto the back patio to take one last look around, say goodbye to the lovely oasis. I knocked into a chair. almost sending it to the ground. Righting the chair I took time to enjoy the vibrant garden surrounding me. A large airy dragonfly with gossamer wings turned with each breath of the breeze. A cluster of butterflies was still aglow in dawn's light. Ladybugs, artistically created, were perched on plant branches and in flowerpots, some clustered like a family. Twinkling, colorful sun-catchers hung from the pergola. Aunt Sally's artistry brought the patio and garden to life, fully. I fingered the smooth surface of an aqua blue and orange tweedy bird. I took it off the hook to dangle it from my hand, then unconsciously placed it in my pocket as I sat down.

Coffee sloshed over the edge of the mugs as Aunt Sally stormed out of the house toward me.

"What are you doing" she demanded as she slammed the mugs on the wrought iron bistro table, losing even more coffee.

Looking down at the half empty coffee mugs, then up at my aunt in puzzlement, I replied, "I didn't break it."

"Break what?"

I stood up. "The chair, the silly chair. It just tipped over, but I caught it." I carefully lowered myself onto the chair, hoping to come across as calm and unconcerned and therefore diminishing my aunt's fury. *What was up with her anyway.*

Speaking slowly as if to a child, my aunt sounded like a schoolteacher about to give me detention, "I am not talking about a chair." Her voiced raised, "And you know it!"

Almost automatically, my hand fell to my pocket. Aunt Sally's eye followed, "What do you mean?" I sputtered lamely.

"Oh puleeeez!"

"Um tweedy?" I removed it from my pocket and placed the small offender on the table between us. A peace offering.

"Yes, the bird. My. Bird. You stole my bird. You could have just asked for it." Aunt Sally's voice was still strained.

My response came up to her challenge. "Oh, so I could have had it, but because I have it, then I stole it. That makes no sense. Keep your stupid bird." I wanted to slam it on the table but it was too cute, I didn't want to break it.

"Stupid bird. Sure, stupid. What about your actions? I give you a place to stay, to curl up and hide from the world and you suddenly say good bye. Oh. Oh. And on the way out, you steal my sun-catcher. No asking. No warning. Just bye and pocket the bird." Tears, anger, hurt streamed down Aunt Sally's face, mirroring the tears on my face.

We looked at each other through our tears and instantly were in each other's arms. "I'm sorry Aunty Sally. Really. I uh, I don't know. It was just there looking so irresistible".

"No, it's me. Watching you in anguish all these months was almost too much. You would think I would be happy to see you venturing out. And I am, truly I am. And then, do you take me with you? Noooo, you take the dang bird!"

"Tweedy." I offered lamely.

With her face against mine as we embraced, I felt Aunt Sally's cheek rise, signaling a smile. Releasing her, I asked, "Can I take Tweedy? It would be like having you along with me."

"I've been replaced by a piece of decor. Well it is handcrafted so yes, Tweedy along with you."

CHAPTER FIVE

The Frog

AND THE PRINCE

After breakfast, Aunt Sally straightened up in the kitchen as I came in to hug her goodbye. She followed me out. I placed my furry companion in her blanket on the passenger seat and climbed into the driver's seat. Aunt Sally walked around the van, video rolling, to the driver's window. She put the phone in her bright multi-colored bathrobe pocket. "Ok kiddo, get out and give me one last hug."

As I reached for the door handle, the full impact of my aunt's bathrobe hit me. "Wow Aunt Sally, that's one bright robe!" It screamed riotous-color.

Stepping back, Aunt Sally swayed, letting her colorful robe dance before my eyes. "I made it last night. If you stay, I will make you one!" A conspiring smile lit up her face.

"Um. No, and no. Not my style, though it is a work of art. Where did you get those lime-colored buttons?"

"Chartreuse my dear." Sally wrapped her arms around. "Be safe. And everything else."

"Yes, and everything else."

A surge of release coursed through me as I hopped back into my camper van, ruffled the top of Peaches' head and turned the key to start my life. I told myself that the first few steps were the most difficult, but the next 1800 miles would be less complicated. I was ready to face the "everything else" Aunt Sally had mentioned.

I carefully backed out of the driveway, glancing around at the garden art that lined the driveway bursting with Aunt Sally's creative expressions.

Just as I got to the end of the driveway, I saw the frog that represented Uncle Drake, my aunt's one and only true love. Uncle Drake's life ended suddenly by a car that ran a red light. There was more to the story of the frog. Aunt Sally had always giggled and said one day she would tell me the saga of how the frog came to represent Uncle Drake.

Aunt Sally was standing in the courtyard by the front door, watching me leave. I waved her closer as I called out, "What about the frog?"

"What?" Aunt Sally asked, coming toward me so she could hear over the engine noise.

"The frog." I called out. "You never told me the story of the frog."

A big grin took over my aunt's face. "I'll tell you. But that will take a cup of coffee. Which means your new life will have to be put on hold for a little longer."

If Aunt Sally's grin was the bait, I was hooked. I kind of thought the grin wasn't my aunt stalling, but her memory of the frog and Uncle Drake. I pulled the van forward a bit, parked it under a tree to provide shade, turned off the engine and glanced at my sleeping companion. Peaches looked comfy. I rolled down the windows to catch any breeze and climbed out of the camper. My curiosity was stronger than my need to be on the road. The "everything else" could wait a few more minutes.

As I was exiting my camper, Aunt Sally turned toward the seating area in her courtyard saying, "Get comfy, I'll be right out."

Another tree keep the courtyard cool and thankfully the sun was still making its way over her condo. I went to the elaborately crafted piece of leafy, swirling metal artwork that served as a table between two chairs. Yes, Aunt Sally had made it. As I admired it I sat down, pulling several pillows out from behind me. Being tall meant I never needed pillows to bolster me up.

My aunt came back out carrying two fresh mugs of coffee; handing one to me as she sat down, still grinning.

"Ok," I ventured, "Uncle Drake was your prince that came forth when you kissed a frog!"

"Nope."

"What? Uncle Drake wasn't your knight in shining armor." I exclaimed in mocked horror.

"My dear girl, did you ever see him when he came out from under a Maserati after working on it all day? Shining is not a word I would use for your uncle."

"Ok. No more guesses. Tell me."

"Well, the first thing you need to know is that your uncle was not ticklish."

"I know that Aunt Sally. I remember all the times I tried to get back at him when he was tickling me. It never worked. How does tickling relate to a frog?"

"Patience, my dear niece…"

Sally looked at the crisp blue sky, then back down at the mug she held. She took a sip, sighed, then began, "Drake was not ticklish unless he got the hiccups. His hiccups were a masterpiece. A very loud masterpiece. A full throttled masterpiece. The only way to halt the racket was to tickle him."

"One of our last play-dates was an evening art walk in downtown on a brisk fall night. All the studios participated. Each served little nibblies along with wine, coffee or hot cocoa. Did I say wine? Drake and I made our outing a wine tasting, art walk combination. It wasn't the plan, but we forgot to nibble. All wine, no nibbles."

Sally looked at me with a mischievous grin. Knowing my aunt and uncle were light drinkers, I nodded, "And you got tipsy?"

"Well, we were more than halfway through the walk and we could still navigate between all the people, mostly. Let's say we were pleasantly mellow and a touch silly. One more sip of wine would have been one too many."

I chuckled, knowing that my aunt could get giddy with just a whiff of a newly opened bottle of wine. "Did Uncle Drake have to hold you steady?"

"It was a joint effort. The Tee Pee method. We both leaned into each other. I'm sure we looked like lovebirds." That grin again. "That's when we entered Beyond the Gnome. You know the garden art store on Main in the historic Towne Plaza? Historic, meaning it had a narrow door and lots of tight spaces."

I nodded.

"Just as we walked in, Drake hiccupped. Loudly! I leaned into him and he took a wobbly step backwards, almost bumping into the people right behind us. He stepped forward with another boisterous hiccup. I wanted to get us out of the store because, well, his loud hiccups and people were waiting to enter. His noisy hiccups were so embarrassing. But he wanted to go in and softly nudged me back through the door."

Aunt Sally imitated his loud hiccup noise. "Again, that jarring hiccup noise. It was time for drastic measures; time to tickle him. Holding his breath never worked, gulping down water always failed. Only tickling did it. I did what I had to do; reached my hands under his jacket and around to the tender spot on his side where I tickled him."

Sally paused, seeing the story unfold in her mind. "Uncle Drake looked down at me in utter confusion. He is pushing my hands away, trying to stop me, looking at me like I've gone bonkers. He asked, *'What are you doing? Stop Sally.'* But I'm ignoring him, swaying around, trying to get a good tickle going to stop his hiccups. We're halfway in the door, then out, then in again, holding up foot traffic as Drake burst forth his booming noises. Like a herd of bullfrogs on speed.

He tries to push me away again. Exasperated, I say, "I'm trying to help you stop your hiccups."

He looks at me as he takes hold of my hands and nods toward the floor, saying, "It's not me Sally, it's that frog statue!" He started swinging his foot forward and back and I heard the frog hiccup, or croak with each movement of Drake's foot.

"Oh, it's the frog! Whoops." I removed my hands from his, straightened out his jacket and laughed.

"We would have collapsed into each other's arms laughing except for the small crowd of people we had held up as they were stepping in and out of the store. I looked at the curious and somewhat perturbed faces around us and mumbled, 'It's the frog.' "

Drake turned me around and guided us out of the doorway onto the sidewalk, hearing the comments of the people held back by our antics. It was nice that some of them laughed. Truly, we barely noticed those with perturbed faces. We collapsed onto a bench in unrestrained laughter. The wine might have helped."

Aunt Sally was laughing just thinking about that day. I couldn't help but join her. Sally continued, "After Drake died, oh maybe a month later, I was in a fog wandering around downtown in the middle of the week. It was cavernously empty. I didn't know why I was even there or where I was going. I just needed to get out of the house. I didn't even know I was at Beyond the Gnome as I sleep-walked through the door. Then I heard the loud hiccup, the croaking frog. Uncle Drake's hiccup."

Aunt Sally stopped, breathed, then took a long, slow sip of coffee, just to do something as the memories rushed back, bringing a flush to her face. "Losing Drake was devastating. He was too young to be taken from me, too full of life." Her voice was softer when she continued. "I remember wanting so badly to have one more moment with him, one more touch.

I kept praying, begging God; 'Let me feel him, his caress.' I never got to say goodbye. I cried out often, a prayer from deep within my soul asking, 'Lord, is my Drake with you? Is he ok? Please let me know.' "

When I walked through that door and heard his hiccups, I felt like God had answered my prayers, like Drake was right there with me. The sound of us laughing on that bench soothed my heart and filled me with a measure of peace. I just sunk down to the floor right next to the frog and sat there, moving my hand up and down in front of the frog to make it hiccup. That loud croaking. Ribbit. Ribbit. It was Drake's hiccups."

Sally's eyes glistened with unshed tears. As I reached out and took my aunt's hand, Sally said, "I'm alright. It's a memory that will never leave me. It was a light amid my wretched tunnel of grief."

A moment passed. With a strange smile, maybe like the ones you save for the senile, she said, "Oh, and it was the ugliest frog I had ever seen!"

After a deep drink from her cup, she went on. "The store clerk came over; she was younger, a twenty-something woman. She had such a curious look on her face. I learned later she was the owner's daughter. She helped her mom run the store. Standing, looking down at me, she said with hesitation, 'Can I help you?' I mean, there I was, a grown woman on the floor playing with this ugly frog and crying. I *bet* she thought I needed help!"

I stood up and pointed at the frog, saying, "I want to buy this."

"Oh, it's not for sale. It lets us know when someone comes into the store."

"You don't understand," I responded, sniffing back my tears. I shared my story with her. With both our eyes dripping tears of laughter and sorrow, she guided me to a lively painted bench back by the register, sat me down, got me a glass of water and a tissue. "Let me check something in my catalog."

A few minutes later, she came back smiling. "I found him, another frog." She sat down next to me and showed me a picture like the frog at the door, but not as ugly. "I'd be glad to order this for you." She offered.

Her kindness touched me. You forget sometimes that perfect strangers can touch you with a simple act when your hurting. I looked toward the door, then back at the catalog. "Um, could I buy the one in the catalog but take the one at the door?" I asked.

She looked at me confused, "But that one is pretty beat up....and kind of ghastly."

"Exactly."

I didn't need to say anything more. She understood, walked to the front door, picked up the battered, hiccupping frog and returned, as she asked, 'Would you like him in a bag or gift wrapped?'

She went back to previewing the catalog. "Ok. I can get this brand new, unscarred one by tomorrow. Let me warp up your treasure."

I responded, "His name is Drake and I know just where to put him."

Since then, Drake has been forever crouched at the foot of the driveway, watching over all who come and go while belting out hiccups as they do so. That silly frog is a reminder of how much Drake loved to laugh and how faithful God was in answering my pleadings."

I sat stone still, recognizing the unspoken needs within my own heart. Aunt Sally got up, walked over and put her arms around me, "You will find answers, Jani. Maybe not all the answers you want, but there is life beyond your tragedy. You will find it. That is my prayer for you while you travel to Dungeness."

"Thank you, Aunt Sally. I'm ready to find those answers."

CHAPTER SIX

Calling

MY PARENTS

As Aunt Sally and I walked toward the van she gently urged, "I totally support you in doing this trip. I know this will be healing for you, but Jani, I feel it is important to talk to your parents."

My faint nod of consent had Aunt Sally's fingers pressing speed dial. Maybe my parents would be so far off the grid they'd have no cell service. I could almost hear Aunt Sally praying that her nomadic sister and her brother-in-law were near a cell tower. I got in the van to assure myself that no one could dissuade me.

Oh no! The phone rang. Sally put the call on Facetime. "Hey Sally," I heard my dad say cautiously, "Everything ok?"

Sally didn't know how to begin. She shifted so that I was visible. "Brian, is Pam there? Janine and I would like to share something with the both of you."

My father squinted into the phone. "What are you sitting in, Janine? Did you buy a car?"

"No, Dad, a camper van. I'm um. I'm. Well, I'm taking a trip."

"Wait honey, let me get your mother."

We heard him call over his shoulder. I saw my mom come up behind him as Dad explained, "Janine bought a camper van and is planning a trip."

They turned toward the screen and in unison asked, "Where are you headed?"

"Dungeness Spit, Daddy, Mom." I said into the smart phone to my used-to-be sophisticated father. My dad's face was not the one I had grown up with. This unfamiliar face hid behind bushy facial hair and a ponytail. *When did dad go 60s hippie?*

"Dungeness?" he said, trying to keep the alarm out of his voice. The expression in his eyes spoke the words he was trying not to say. I knew he had longed to hear my voice speaking in full sentences. Until this day, my speaking was mostly just dull sounds in response to his calls any time he attempted to reach out to me. I could tell he didn't quite like what he was hearing, but I was talking and the relief started to showed on his face.

"Yes, Dungeness." I responded with shaky resolve.

Why had I let Aunt Sally make the call? I merely wanted to be on the road driving, not trying to hide my trembling voice as I gaped, a bit mystified, at my transformed father. Kenny Rogers? Sean Connery? Jason Momoa but older?

Whoever he was, I saw him nod, his attempt to understand my decision, as his eyes became moist. To avoid having me notice, he hurriedly handed the phone to my mother. I saw my mother's face full of questions that yearned for answers. In truth, I couldn't answer all the questions either. My mother had transformed as well. Sure enough, as my mom pulled the phone back, I saw the era that my mom now represented. *Who sells granny dresses anymore? Oh wait; this was probably my mom's handiwork, an original granny dress! Go figure. The 60s had overtaken both my parents.*

The last time I had seen my mom was when my parents had stopped their never-ending road trip at Aunt Sally's to hug me, though I was pretty much non-responsive. At that time, my mother had flowers cascading down the back of her hair; her long, graying, uncolored hair. It was no longer the professionally cut and styled short business woman's hair. Flowers. "They match the pattern in my dress." My mom had pronounced with forced gaiety, turning around so I could get the full impact of the ensemble. I stared with dull eyes. Huh?

What my mother was really trying to do was force some lightness into my hollowed dark life. It didn't work. And, like the few other visits, the awkward silence made everyone uncomfortable. As family dynamics went, they were like a corral of skittish horses desperate to break free of the fencing, knocking into each other as they sought escape, with too much misdirected energy. Thankfully, it ended after a brief interlude, as my parents found the open gate and fled my room. Relieved, I would turn over in my bed and hunker down under the covers with Peaches. Aunt Sally would quietly shut the guest room door. I covered my ears with a pillow to avoid all the hushed questions spoken in worrisome tones.

There I was, ready to leave my aunt's place but I was forced to chat with my parents. Attempting to sound strong, I spoke, "I'm leaving Aunt Sally's place to go on a road trip." It was really more of a mumble. I tried to explain further, "Well, I was out driving a week ago and I got lost. Then I found this van for sale. I...well...I bought it."

My hippie parents were not quite ready to give in. "Oh Jani," my mother implored, using my nickname, "Are you sure? Can't we sort through this with you?" I saw my mother turn to look at my dad, asking him, "How quickly can we get to Mesa, honey?

"Mom. Dad. No. Please don't come."

I saw immediately that they wouldn't take "no" for an answer.

Panic gripped me. I just wanted to go. I needed to go without all this interference. Their parental fretfulness smothered me under a towering mound of wet autumn leaves. I put more resolved in my voice, "I'll be gone. I'm leaving right now."

Then I saw the painful expression on my mother's face. It made me soften. "Mom, I'm ok, really. I'm done sorting. There is no such thing.

I need to do this." I handed the phone back to my aunt. The two sisters, Aunt Sally and my mom, just stared blankly at each other, the lines of age, sorrow and worry etched on their faces. Neither knew what to say or what to do.

I, who had always been the light of my parents' world, had become a recluse. I had isolated myself ever since providence had unleashed destruction upon my neatly arranged, yet meaningful, life. In a moment's time, the joyous glow of the sun breaking through on a cloudy day that had always been me, turned into a turbulent storm. At its center was a sullen, tormented person they could not reach. The darkness had stolen my life, my breath, my reason to live. All too quickly I was gone. Over. Destroyed.

I saw my mother fretting, trying to find a reason to stop me from what seemed like, to her, an impulsive plan. Meanwhile, the only thing I knew was that this camper van was the way to reclaim my life.

I wasn't ready to deal with the look of apprehension engraved on my parents' faces. That was too much weight to shoulder. *Why aren't they happy? I am trying to find my way back to being alive.*

My dad's face came on the screen. After inhaling slowly he said, as Aunt Sally turned the phone more toward me, "Jani, I think this is good for you."

"Don't tell her that, Brian." I heard my mother gasp.

As Aunt Sally held the phone, I watched my parents, one after the other, as they jostled for face-time. Even with my thoughts miles down the road, the pain I heard in their words and held within their eyes, struck me. *They've been hurting too?* I thought.

Seeing this just about broke my resolve. I felt like I was being swallowed back into the murky shadow of desperation; that clinging, frightening hollowness that had suffocated my soul for far too long.

No! I thought, *No! I could not go there. I did not want to go back to that clawing darkness.*

When I spoke again, it was with a heart full of conviction, "Mom, I have to go. It's time for me to face what happened. Something inside of me is pressing me forward." With determination, I continued, "Until I do this, I can't do anything else. I'm just wasting away here."

I looked apologetically at my aunt, who was leaning in just outside of the driver's window where I sat.

"Sorry Aunt Sally. You've been so good to me."

"No...no... don't worry about me. Like I said, I feel this is good for you. Go do what you have to do." Then Sally spoke to her sister, my mom, "Pam, you remember how my life was after Drake died? At first, I was helpless...hopeless. Finally, something kicked me in the tush and made me live again. No, not something, someone...you dear sis. Now Jani is being pushed to live again."

Sally wiped her tear-streaked face using the arm of her bathrobe. She smiled with determination and looked straight into the phone at her sister. "Seems to me that my big sister kept nudging me every time I wanted to float down that river called denial. Jani is ready for this, Pam." With a tentative smile, Sally tried to lighten the mood. "Let's look at this camper Jani is going to be driving."

With the phone in her hand, my aunt went around to the passenger door, opened it up and peered in past the seat, using her phone to show my parents what she was looking at. "Hmmm, nice lookin' rig." She glanced over at me. "Want some company?"

Just then Peaches uncurled herself from her bedding on the passenger seat and responded with a yap. *"Uh excuse me. I'm here, ya know! What more company does Janine need?!"*

I stretched over and petted Peaches to forestall a yap-fest. Aunt Sally said, "Oh, you have the killer dog staking out her territory already?"

"Yes, Aunt Sally, I am well protected." To affirm my statement, Peaches gave Sally her most disdainful snort, which to the mere human ear sounded like a sniffle.

I reached for the phone in Sally's hand and looked at my parents. "It's time for me to do this." Then I scanned the face of my aunt, who had loved me beyond words and had helped me to get out of bed on good days for many months and I said to all of them, "I'll call in a few days. I have to go now or I'll lose my nerve."

Both my parents nodded with reluctant acceptance. I tried to smile as I spoke, "I'm following your lead Mom.... Dad. I'm going off the grid."

Their responding smiles held the weight of worry. Gently my father consoled his wife, "Pam," he spoke softly, "Jani needs to go. How many nights have you cried over all that has happened? How that day robbed her of all that meant anything to her? She has to go." Watching his face, I imagined he didn't know if he was trying to reassure my mom or bolster his own heavy heart.

"Yes. Okay, Jani. I wish it could be... well, I just wish that we could be there with you. But yes, go sweetheart." Mom put her fingers to her lips, then touched the screen. "Keep her safe, Lord. Make her path straight." I saw her soundless lips say, Amen.

"Go Jani. We'll be praying." Dad said. We hung up with everyone in a better frame of mind, albeit emotionally sapped, like a tree in spring; gooey, sticky stuff running out all over, but still standing.

"Oh, I almost forgot." Sally reached into her bathrobe pocket and pulled out a small, folded piece of paper that was torn from her journal and handed it to me. I meant to give this to you before you left; I came across it this morning while reading in Psalms.

I unfolded the paper and read what my aunt had written; *Psalm 56:3 "When I am afraid, I will put my trust in You."*

She said, "We can't always see where the road leads, but God promises he is walking right along with us. We just have to trust Him."

"Thanks Aunt Sally. I haven't looked at scripture in a while. I'll keep this where I can see it."

"Looks like the killer dog is getting impatient." My aunt said.

With that, we hugged once more through the window. I turned the key, put the van in reverse and slowly took my foot off the brake that had stopped my life. It was time to be on my way. I petted Peaches' little snout, "I'm ready to find some answers, little girl."

Peaches sighed, curled up, and went back to sleep.

Then it hit me. I pressed on the brake, opened my window and projected my voice over the running motor to Aunt Sally. "I am searching for my life."

I looked back over my shoulder, down the driveway, "I am doing this by driving backwards. That's about right. I need to go back before I can go forward."

"I get it Jani, I really do." Aunt Sally responded as she waved me off, "Go on now...get moving."

CHAPTER SEVEN

Dear

READER

A mere five weeks before this, I had still been more or less unresponsive, huddled in Aunt Sally's guest bedroom, not taking part in life. I now sat in a camper van, ready to hit the road. I knew Aunt Sally had prayed for the right words to bring healing to me, her broken niece. But nothing seemed to help. Nothing. Now I was driving off. Was this a good thing? An answer to my aunt's prayer. Or was this insanity? Maybe something in between?

I know I keep referring to my tragedy and my dismal state of being. I don't mean to string you along. It's just really hard to talk about it. Let me spit it out. My daughter, or rather our daughter, since I was married to Ken at the time, was six when we were camping at the Dungeness Spit on the Olympic Peninsula. There was a terrible accident that took her life. My baby. She was singing gleefully one minute; in the next minute she was gone.

I'm sorry, I can't do this. I mean, that is what this trip is about, right? Rooting out all the feelings I've stuffed down, hoping this unbearable pain will ease. This will not be painless. I get that. But, oh man, this is harder than I thought it would be.

My head is spinning. I'll try to explain more to you, maybe a bit later.

Okay. I admit it.

I can't wait until my baby shower.

I bought a baby book. I had to.

I felt our little one kick me today.

Keep kicking little one, 'til daddy gets home.

Chapter Nine

Briefly Ken

I'm not good at words. I'm not ready to write. I love Janine. Always have. Always will.

Yes, I let her go when she asked for a divorce, because I love her. If that would have helped her heal, then I would do it. Here's something I haven't shared with anyone. I never signed the final divorce papers. I waited. After a while when no one asked for them, I thought I'd leave it that way. I don't even know if she knows. We didn't use lawyers; Janine found a document online, and that was it.

Maybe I can write a little at a time. It was Danny, my brother-in-law, who suggested this. He said journaling would be good for me. For a first attempt, this wasn't so bad.

CHAPTER TEN

Before

DESOLATION STRUCK

Janine, as a little girl, was a long and lean child. When she walked into her eight-grade homeroom trying to hold her head up, though nerves were threatening to make her slouch, there were no other kids in the class. Not at her eye level, anyway. Like a giraffe, she had to bend and dip to make eye contact with her peers. She was the tallest person in her class since kindergarten. In her junior year, she peaked at 5'10". That is also when she reached her athletic stride while still fighting to tame her short golden hair. Her moss-green eyes missed very little, which added to her athletic prowess. She was acutely aware of the action around her. Janine and her brother Danny were born and raised in the Pacific Northwest on Whidbey Island. As an outdoor person, she thrived in the mild island temperatures that allowed for hiking vigorously up a mountain or taking a long challenging bike ride on the hilly, curving, scenic back roads of the island.

Even on cloudy days, she created her own joy as she snuggled under a throw blanket with a good book, sitting in her father's over-sized recline, all arms and legs sticking out a strange angles. As she got older, she hung out at her favorite cafe sipping a double mocha latte and chatting with almost everyone that came in, easily, espousing her take on current events. She was a planner. Her mom was a planner, but not like Janine who had her whole life mapped out very early on. Like wanting to be a physical therapist. After helping Danny recover from his foot injury. Any little ouch or strained muscle in the family, Janine was on it. She was relentless, though tender, mostly.

As a small-town girl, there was also an undercurrent that tugged her toward the city. That draw would play itself out after high school. Janine had grown up feeling safe; never having to be warned about who she could or couldn't talk to, which, for an outgoing child, suited her perfectly. She spent her early years embraced by the luxury that came from familiarity, from living in a community where she knew just about everyone. There were no strangers in Janine's world.

Her parents always tried to give Janine and Danny adventuresome experiences. Her mom especially enjoyed changing things up, even if the family wasn't always on board with it. In contrast, one tradition was established, a family camping trip to the Olympic Peninsula. They would explore the rain forests, soak in the natural hot springs at Sol Duc, and walk the beaches at Neah Bay, picking up sand dollars. Danny loved Neah Bay, but for Janine, the outings to Dungeness Spit were always her favorite. The rhythm of the pounding surf as the family walked the trail on the bluff above the Straits of Juan de Fuca, resonated deep within her. The sturdy hemlock trees and wiggly branched madrone trees always caught her attention. She named many of them. Janine would dream and plan and animatedly share her thoughts as they wandered down the trail to the water. Danny would run, throw stones over the cliff, climb the fences and egg on his sister to stop her chattering, imploring her to play with him.

They would often look down at the people below on horseback, riding along the rough beach, the surf frolicking at hoofs as they cantered by. Nighttime meant the family made their way down to the beach to join others around a campfire. If they were the first there, they built the fire. As people gathered, everyone would sing, laugh, roast s'mores and talk until a sleepy Janine and Danny drifted off. Her parents learned the first year at the Spit, that carrying sleeping children back up the steep incline was arduous work. Where's a horse when you need it? From thereafter, at the first signs of the kids nodding, they'd roust them and all four would walk back up to the campsite.

It gave her parents a sense of hope and satisfaction to see Janine grow into a young woman, secure in who she was. As her high school years were ending, the other side of Janine emerged. She had always shown drive and ambition on the softball field as in any of her other outdoor pursuits. She was highly competitive, winning often but enjoying the game no matter what the score was at the end. To Janine, life was at its best when she was going, doing, running, riding, swimming or playing hard.

As a high school junior, they saw their daughter's drive, that competitive nature. It compelled her toward the city; a bigger playing field with more opportunities to compete. After receiving acceptance from several colleges, her parents supported Janine's choice to attend the University of Washington in Seattle. The UW was just a short ferry ride from the island but seemed to answer her big-city curiosities. Janine's decision was confirmed when they all visited the campus. She came alive as they toured the university. It was obvious that this was where Janine needed to be.

Once classes started, she embraced each day with vivacity and determination. The university, dorm life, the city, the learning, all nourished Janine's spirit. Whidbey Island was home to hundreds of eagles that soared overhead daily. That was Janie at the UW. She soared. Like the eagles back home she called out in exhilarating joy as the winds of newness carried her.

She was where she was meant to be.

CHAPTER ELEVEN

Ah Ha

MOMENTS

As I sat behind the wheel of my camper van, packed with pieces of who I used to be, I also realized I must battle with my old self to triumph. It took too long for me, hiding out at my Aunt Sally's house in Mesa, to decide I wanted to fight the chains that kept my heart bound in desolation.

As I maneuvered the twists and turns, red lights and stop signs and the mid-week traffic to leave Mesa, my mind was flooded with images.

It felt like it was time to sweep the crumbled remnants of my pain into a pile. Taking one last look at the shattered parts of who I had become, I moved toward the trash can where I dumped it out for collection.

To move forward I had to allow the debris to be tossed away and replaced with something I couldn't yet comprehend. I wanted a life. I knew it had to begin where it had all ended, Dungeness Spit where my little girl died. I knew I had to go back to what used to be my favorite place. It had become the unending nightmare that had destroyed my existence.

I felt empowered as I considered what had happened over the past weeks. I bought the camper van; I had announced that I was leaving Mesa [even if it was with wavering confidence] and I was heading to Washington. I said my farewells and even spoke with my parents. When all the talking, explaining, and question-dodging was done, I put the van in reverse, looked back over my shoulder and pressed on the gas. Moving.

Dungeness Spit...

Where it began...where it ended...

Where I hold out hope that I can begin again.

I was in motion....

driving...

on a road...

not knowing what would happen...

but needing to keep my foot on the gas pedal.

I was wearing my favorite, well broken-in running shoes. I could do it.

I reached over to pet Peaches, put a CD in the slot. Yup it's an older van and I had a few CDs, go figure. I settled back into the driver's seat. I liked the feel of the van on the road. It handled well and rode quietly. Still in Arizona, the sun was shining brightly, its warmth penetrated the van giving me a radiant sense of well-being. I opened my window to create a breeze rather than use the a/c. What breeze? I quickly shut the window and turned on the a/c.

As I came toward an overpass, I noticed it had 3D metal art spanning the entire structure. The wide shoulder, as well, had artwork. Quails. I love quails. As I got closer, I saw the momma quail with little baby quails following, like stepping-stones, each smaller than the one in front of it. The smallest was lagging behind a bit. Momma and her babies.

And just like that the emotional seesaw I was on, slammed to the ground. I was barely ten minutes outside of Mesa, when I had to pull over onto the side of the road. I was crying. My handwritten list of where I would stop, that was in my lap, was a puddle of blue ink. As the sobs abated, I took a few slow deep breaths then crumpled the ruined list, tossing it in the back. Petting Peaches, as I starred at the momma and baby quails, I murmured,

"I hadn't realized mom and dad were hurting also. And Aunt Sally being there as I remained non-responsive. When had I become so blind?"

Peaches, wise as ever, tilted her head, *"Tell me all about it."* Then she placed a paw on my arm. *"I'm with you girl."*

After a few minutes and a few deep breathes, my composure returned. As I was about to get back on the road my cell phone rang. Caller ID let me know that it is my brother Danny. My heart felt a swell of relief.

"Hey bro…" My voice husky from crying.

"Hey Jani," He said, "What are you doing? I just got off the phone with Mom who was going on about you and a van and finding yourself. Taking Peaches; heading to the Spit of all places. It's like one day you're curled up in the fetal position and the next you've been born; popped out into the world, but you're an alien."

I tried to get a word in, to stop him, but my brother hadn't taken a breath in years. I half listened as he went on about something. Then I realized there was dead silence. "Danny?"

"Yup… still here. I was just giving you the mom-version of things. Me? This is sooo cool Jani. You should have hit the road months ago!"

"Uh, really?"

"Stunned ya into silence. Now there's one for the record books. Jani left speechless. Yes, really. This is great. What route are you taking?"

"Well, um, I just cried all over my notes, so all my plans ran together. I may be lost." I said as I glanced around looking for a road sign.

"Well, no biggie. You either go north first or you go west then north. I say, go west, toward the ocean. Then you can stop and see your favorite brother!"

"You're my only brother."

"Makes the "fave" decision easier for you."

"I know, I know. But Danny, it seems like this is something I have to do alone. Just me and getting to my destination. A solitude thing. Later there will be time for visiting."

"Well, I don't get all that, but whatever you have to do to start living again, do it!"

A moment of silence brought a sense of affirmation. It filled me.

"Hey sis, I got a guy waiting with a bunch of food to deliver to the homeless shelter. Gotta go before things wilt."

"Yes, Father Dan, go do the Lord's work." I was reluctant to have the conversation end. My brother's enthusiasm had invigorated my resolve. I imagined that same enthusiasm, as an Anglican Priest, attracted and inspired many people in his congregation. I figured just a few minutes with Father Dan and even the most hardcore person caught his zeal; they'd take out their checkbooks ready to write a check or actually roll up their sleeves and get to work on whatever project needed doing. He had the impact on people ever since high school.

"Love ya, sis."

"You too Danny."

I picture Danny as I'd last seen him. We had walked along the beach with the slow melody of waves singing at our feet and the sun making him squint. Now he was Father Danny. Who would have thought and yet I can see it perfectly.

CHAPTER TWELVE

It's Not

ALL EASY

Looking at Google Maps, I mulled over possible routes. I had some choices. I could have headed to the Valley of Fire which really interested me. I recalled a coffee table book at my aunt's place with stunning photos of the many different hikes across unique terrains at the Valley of Fire. The campground there may be a good first stop.

A wrong turn made the decision for me. I stayed overnight in Indian Springs. The cerulean blue sky was accented with wispy clouds, their softness bringing cottony comfort to my heart. Pulling into an inviting RV park, I decided not to hook up the van. For that one night I made a light salad, walked Peaches and stoppped for the day. I read a little bit then slept hard. Awaking early, fully rested, I was ready for a full day of travel.

The second night I registered at the EZ Breezee RV park near Burns, Oregon. Never heard of it. This was really my second RV park that day. I drove into and right out of a campground that had the feel of a squatter's village or a drug den on wheels. Creeped me out. EZ Breezee was neat, clean and, as I quickly learned, very friendly. I was greeted by Millie when I walked into the office to register.

"Hello young lady, welcome to EZ Breezee, where life doesn't get any better than this." A cheerful Millie announced with certainty. "Will you be staying long?" said this sizable round woman with smiling-eyes, oversized dangling red earrings and thick rimmed Zebra stiped glasses sitting on a petite nose, not to be outdone by her crimson lips.

"Hi...thanks. No. I'll just be here for the night."

"Oh, what a shame, most people just hate to leave." Millie replied, her face open and welcoming, "Well, you can always change your mind. People do that too. They just love being here what with the pool, the trails, the bike paths along the river. Oh, but there I go rambling, again. Let me get you checked in. Let's see..." She pulled out a flyer and a registration card, "Does your camper have hook ups for water, sewer and electric?"

"Yes, it does. It's got it all." I said with pride of ownership. "It's small and easy to drive yet it has full hook ups. Best of all, it has a mini shower, small but I think I can manage it."

"Great. Then let's put you in space #34. That's close to the restrooms, just in case, and it has a nice tree that offers some shade and privacy."

"Sure." I agreed as I tried to recall all my camping trips when I was so particular about what I wanted in a campsite I would inhabit. *Oh heck, I don't remember. Besides, it doesn't really matter.*

"I do have a dog, Peaches. Is that okay?" I asked.

"Hmmm, a dog you say..." Hearing the word dog, a wet nose poked out from the office door behind Millie and woofed once. "There we go. Approval has been given." Millie chuckled. "Come on out Reno and say hello." Turning back to me she asked, "Big?"

"Oh, yes and very vicious. Peaches is a 6-pound Yorkie." I smiled up at Millie as Reno came around to be petted.

"Six pounds. She just made it under our weight limit I'd say." Millie smiled warmly.

Millie liked the young woman in front of her though she did glimpse sadness in her eyes which prompted Millie to want to give her a big hug.

She held back or at least the counter between them held her back. For now, she would let Reno bestow a little love on the young woman as he wagged his tail rapidly in response to the Janine's hands massaging him just behind his ears.

"I'll get my hubby, George. He'll you show you to site #34"

"Oh, I can find it…" I began, but Millie raised her hand, palm out.

"No…no…here at EZ Breezee we give our visitors, our friends, the royal treatment. We always escort them." She winked, "Besides George loves meeting our new EZ Breeze quests." Millie smiled broadly; she loved saying the park's name, even if it was a bit cheesy. Then Millie coughed sharply. "Ahem." she coughed again a bit louder. "AHEM!"

When no response came from the man fiddling around in the back office, Millie hit the "ring for service" bell twice. George perked right up. In walked a beanstalk tall, slender man, slightly bent forward with a worn face that had survived the elements. His chocolate-brown eyes melted away any apprehension someone might have about him.

"George…this is…" She glanced down at the registration form, "Janine. She's just staying one night, well until she changes her mind, of course. She's in #34. Can you escort her there?"

"Why sure thing Sweets. Welcome, Janine. Where ya from?" George asked as he opened the door wide and with a swoop of his arm waved Janine out.

"You stay Reno." He said to his eager companion.

"Phoenix area. Well, that's where I've been for the past year. I'm headed back to Washington."

"Now that's a trip. The wife and I spent about five months there a few years back. Leavenworth area. Beautiful state. What part you going to?"

"I'm headed to the Olympic Peninsula. I grew up on Whidbey Island though."

"Oh, Whidbey, isn't that where the naval base is?"

"Yes, that's right. That's on the north end of the island. I grew up on the south end in Langley."

George scrunched up his furrowed face, thinking, "Ah yes, the artsy town. You an artist?"

"Not really. My dad was the mayor and mom was the city accountant. I was, am a physical therapist. You're right, Langley has some tremendously talented artists living there. Have you ever been?"

George motioned for Janine to get in her van and follow him as he kept up the conversation riding alongside her open window in his golf cart. "No never got that far west. Know a guy who was stationed at the naval base. He and his family always mentioned going to the street fair in Langley. The missus and I are full time workkampers."

"What's a work camper?"

"We travel around the country in our 5th wheel staying in areas anywhere from 3-6 months. To offset campsite fee we work at campgrounds, like this one. We'll be here for another month then we head to Glacier National Park for the summer."

"Wow, really. That sounds like so much fun. Do you have a house somewhere?"

Coming to a Y in the road, George did not answer her last question, but started to guide Janine toward site #34, "You're gonna go to the right up there a bit. It's all one way and 5 mph. Gotta go slowly, we have lots of kiddos."

Janine went pale, taking her foot off the gas pedal. The van stopped moving.

George followed suit, back up to Janine's window and asked. "You okay?"

"Peaches stop it! Oh, sorry, you probably have to piddle." She turned toward George, "I'm sorry what did you say, go left?"

"No, I said, stay to the right. It's all one way and..."

"Got it. Got it." She cut him off before he could say more, "I can find it from here. Thanks though." She gently gave the van some gas. *Watch out for the kiddos.*

"Sure." George said as he carefully swung the cart around giving a last shout, "You need anything just holler."

But Janine was already inching down to the right glancing at the numbers of each site to locate hers Reverberating in her head were George's words, "Watch out for the kiddos."

That wasn't what happened with her sweet Casey.

"Ken."

"Hi lover. Everything okay? You sound energized."

"Sure, sure I'm fine. I'm excited. Can you come home, right now."

Ken was confused, "Wait, what? Sure you're not hurt."

"Casey is about to walk. You have to be here. I'm holding her
on my lap and won't put her down until you get here."

"Casey. Walking!! Hang on to her. I'll be right there."

Chapter Fourteen

Up

and Down

After I drew away from George, I told myself.... *focus... focus. Find the site, let Peaches relieve herself; hook up the water, the sewer and the electric.* Or not. It was just overnight. Yes, it was something to do. I need to do something.

I was mentally going down the setup check list, envisioning everything the previous van owner had shown me. That was my attempt to calm my pounding heart. Strange how simple things seem to trigger me. *"Gotta go slowly, lots of kiddos here..."* Dumb rules that attempts to keep children safe. It is nothing but a lie. Ask me, I know. Liar!! I pounded the side of my fist into the side of the van. Peaches yelped.

How was it that I felt just fine one minute, then the next I was tossed around and thrown down again like a cat playing with a mouse. I wondered if this would ever stop. The sky echoed my mood with dark clouds rolling in from the east quickly swallowing the blue sky.

Sure, now I'll have to walk Peaches in the rain. Or drag her, which is usually the case in wet weather.

Danny's words came to mind reminding me that I was like a pressure cooker. God was opening the vent in restrained degrees to allow my emotional pressure to gradually seep out rather than explode all over the kitchen that is my life.

He painted such descriptive pictures that spoke to me. And the pendulum. In a crisis, he told me to expect that my emotions and thoughts would swing to extremes, far and wide. If I gave it time after a while the arc would become less and less, bringing me to a steadier state. I thought of Newton's pendulum on my science teacher's desk in high school. I loved setting it off, as did most of the kids in my class.

Wait. Did that thing ever stop? Will my wildly fluctuating emotions ever stop? I sure hope Danny knows what he's taking about with all of this.

CHAPTER FIFTEEN

A Caring

COUPLE

Back at the office Millie noticed George's quicker than usual return. He loved to meet and greet campers, chatting up all the visitors and afterwards sharing with her everything he had learned about their travels.

"Back so soon?"

"Janine's originally from Washington…western, heading back that way."

"Uh huh. And?"

"Don't know. It's like she got spooked. She kinda dismissed me. One minute we're talking, the next it's thanks but no thanks."

"Hm. She seemed nice enough." Millie paused remembering Janine's eyes and said, "Yet even through her polite smile I saw a sorrow of some kind. And traveling alone. I know gals do that, but it always makes me wonder."

"Now Sweets, you always wonder. You love to know the inside of people."

"True dear. You do know me, don't you? Should I be concerned about her?" She asked bringing the conversation back to Janine.

"Well, Janine's as safe here as in most campgrounds, Millie. As for her sorrowin', we won't ever know, will we? She'll be gone in the morning."

Millie would be the mother to all who crossed her path but with George's help she had learned to keep that urge under control. Changing the subject, George said, "Well I'd better go crank up the Bar-bee for dinner."

"Oh, I did that. It should be about ready." Millie smiled, she loved pampering George and vice versa.

George came around the counter to head out the office door in the back that led to their 5th wheel and the waiting grill. Thankfully it was undercover. Rain seemed imminent. "Thanks Sweets." He gave Millie a kiss as he passed, "Chicken in a few minutes. You want something to drink?"

"That sounds good. Let me close up the office and I'll prepare some veggies... broccoli sound okay?"

"Sure does."

CHAPTER SIXTEEN

I Am

MOVING FORWARD

At site #34 I was hooked up; Peaches got in a quick walk just as the daunting clouds poured out every drop of water held within their threatening gloominess. We each nibbled away at our dinner safe, warm and dry in our little home on wheels. I read the flyer and brochure the gal at the office had given me.

Although I had only been gone less than two days, I felt worlds away from where I had been for the last year. I had left the desert entering the mountains with its clean crisp air that was invigorating. Ah, and the rain after arid Arizona. There was green all around us and actual water running boisterously somewhere beyond my camp site. In this setting, the prospect of having a life became compelling. I took in another deep breath of fresh moist air before closing the window.

Peaches laid down for a nap after her little walk. I wanted a walk too. No, a run. I peered outside and saw that there was a real possibility the clouds were moving on. This may be the ideal time to rekindle my love of running. I flipped through the campground flyer until I found the a picture of the layout. There it was, a trail along the river where I could run. In another twenty minutes the coast was clear, no more rain. Although the ground was wet, it hadn't gotten mushy.

"I'm going running Peaches." She scrunched down into the bedding. "No, I am not going to make you go with me." Peaches smiled.

Ok, my running shoes... where are they.

I was mentally unpacking my camper trying to remember where I had put things. I found them and went outside the camper to begin stretching my dormant muscles. Once ready, I locked my camper, threw the keys under my rear tire, checked the fitness tracker on my wrist, and stopped short as a chill of familiarity made me shiver.

When I threw my van keys under the front tire, I flashed back to Dungeness. That was what we always did, so whoever got back to the camp site first could get in. The familiarity would have felt good but the edges of pain had not fully receded. I wanted to remember the good parts of my past not have all the sorrow keep pushing into my life.

To find my future, I guess I must stop running from my past first, I told myself, *I should expect the memories to fight each other for prominence. I thought of a mantra to begin my run, "Born to run. Born to run."*

With renewed resolve, finished my stretches, stood up straighter and headed toward the trail. As I pass the 5-mph sign, I deliberately turned my head to avoid the sign, *"Slow. Kids at Play"*.

Outside my kitchen window I see
Casey and Peaches playing in the yard.
Oh wait, Casey has treats in her hand
and is training Peaches saying,
"Twirl Peaches. Like me. Twirl."
Casey is twirling while holding out a treat.
Peaches chases her hand making a circle not a twirl.
Ah, Casey figures it out. She holds still and
makes wide circles above Peaches head with a treat.
Soon Casey and Peaches are running,
stopping and twirling together.
This new trick became the norm when
Peaches greeted someone she knows.
She, and Casey, always wiggling and twirling.
Twins.

CHAPTER EIGHTEEN

Millie

TAKES A WALK

George and Millie were finishing up the dishes when Millie plopped down in a camp chair her huge red earrings swinging and tingling as she did so. "I'm beat." she announced. "I've been on my feet all day. How many people came into the park today, Georgie-boy?"

"More than usual, that's for sure. Ya know I can register them and you could drive around in the cart bringing campers to their sites. Then you wouldn't have to be standing all day long." George came over and sat in the chair next to Millie taking her hand.

"It's not the standing so much as the standing in one place. When I am moving, tidying up or putting brochures on the shelves it doesn't get to me. My leg just stiffens up when I am at that desk for too long."

"I'll try to remember to give you a break on busy days."

Millie smiled at her husband, "Oh? And who will give the poor campers a break when I'm behind the wheel of that cart?"

"Millie, it can only do 8 miles an hour. You can't do too much damage with it."

"Ha! Watch me. I'm an untamed woman." She tossed her head side to side to get her earrings to join in.

"Well untamed woman, why don't you let me help you with your leg and get you comfy?"

"Ya know honey as much as I'd like that; I think I need to take a short walk. Work out some of these kinks."

"Untamed and kinky…my kind of woman! Want some company?"

"Sure, that would be wonderful."

"Okay let me cleanup the BBQ and I'll catch up with you."

Millie, with a bit of effort, got up, gave George a quick peck and headed out the door. "I think I'll head toward the river path. Oh, don't forget to lock up…"

"Yes, I know and I won't forget the pager and to put a note on the door. I'll be there in a quick minute."

As tired as she was, with each step Millie felt the stiffness and pain, that began in her hip and radiated outward to her back, started to abate. She concentrated on her breathing, slowly taking air deep into her lungs then releasing it to the count of ten. As she approached the river, she was thankful that not many people were out walking yet. Usually, she loved to chat and visit with campers, but tonight she wanted a peaceful, uninterrupted walk with George – no need for conversation, just being together strolling along in each other's company.

A little ways down the path Millie noticed a runner coming toward her; it looked like the young woman who had checked in earlier. Millie was contemplating taking the less developed path to her right to preserve her time of quiet when she saw an unleashed dog romp onto the path.

Crumb buns. Where did that dog come from? And where was its owner? That looks like the dog from site 67. Millie thought. *I warned them yesterday about keeping their dog on a leash. Humph.*

Millie loved dogs, but on leashes. Besides, this one was big. Large dogs could intimidate her, in fact, they scared her, what with her bad leg and all.

She could never quite tell if a dog was friendly or not. She felt defenseless knowing a big dog could easily throw her off balance. Feeling uncomfortable, she glanced over her shoulder to see if George was headed her way yet.

Nope, gotta deal with this on my own. She decided to take the other higher path to avoid the dog. As she looked back the dog was gone. Relieved Millie kept walking along the river; no need to divert.

CHAPTER NINETEEN

Leg Work

After doing a few stretches, my running happened in starts and sputters, at a very uneven pace. I was so totally out of shape. Being forced to stop and catch my breath was a good thing. I could absorb the beauty. Oh gosh; there was lush green all around me with babbling water soothing me even as I pushed to get my rhythm back. Shards of light cut through the branches to illuminate the path. It was a good path for running, packed down hard, not a lot of loose rocks to throw me off or trip me up. I could look forward not down as I ran, enjoying the serenity of nature's backdrop.

Out of the corner of my eye I glimpsed a dog halfway beneath a bush, pawing at the ground trying to get to whatever resided underneath the dirt. Nature, water, animals and humans. All parts of life.

Running in place, I looked at my fitness tracker to gauge how far I had run. When I looked up, I saw the large black hairy dog running full bore toward me. Oh my gosh, the dog didn't look that big when it was furiously digging away. It got bigger the closer it got to me. Whether friend or foe it was coming at me fast. Automatically, I tried to make myself look just as hefty by waving my arms and speaking with authority. "Get!" Shooshing my arms outward I commanded, "Go home. Go home."

The dog turned and ran away. I hadn't even noticed the other woman who froze as hulk-dog turned to gallop toward her. A near collision looked about to occur. I tried to call out to the woman. I was too late. The dog swiftly swiped close to the woman and knocked her off balance causing her to awkwardly fall to the ground. Then it bound up and down wanting to play. Instantly, I started to run towards her waving my arms and shooing the dog.

It was the lady that registered me...Mary...Marcie... no Millie, I realized as I heard this chilling scream.

Millie screamed out in pain grabbing her leg. Finally, the dog vaulted off in the opposite direction. I was running to Millie's aid still shouting at the dog to "go home! In case it wanted to change its direction and come back at us.

"Millie... are you okay?" I called out as I neared the woman who was holding her thigh with her leg stretched out. It looked bent, badly wrenched. *Oh no, it was horribly broken!*

They we were on the packed dirt trail, the river singing a peaceful hymn as Millie wailed and rocked rubbing her crooked, terribly shattered leg.

I sat down beside her, "Is it broken? What can I do? Get ice?"

Millie took a breath, let out a long sigh then answered, "It can't break. It's not real. A prosthetic." She gasped in pain and moaned some more.

Embarrassed, she tried to lighten the moment, "When our buddy fido rammed into me, it twisted everything." A deep sob. A choking gasp. She went on. "I need to remove it."

I was trying to take it all in and was unsure of what to do, how to help, "Uh, do you need me to, um, take it off you?"

I've worked with physical therapy clients who had prosthetics. Even though I was hesitant with Millie, I knew I could help her if she wanted me to remove it.

"No just watch out for that dog!" Millie said with vehemence, then groaned again in obvious pain. Slowly she forced herself to start removing her leg.

Once it was off, she let out a long sigh, closing her eyes for a moment. "That helps."

A few minutes later George came leisurely around the bend, unaware that Millie had been hurt. When he saw Millie on the ground he ran to her shouting. "What happened? Are you ok?" Then he bent down to assess Millie's injuries.

Millie was now lying flat on her back waiting for the remaining pain to recede. She reached her hand out to George, "I've been better."

I explained rapidly, "There was a huge black dog. It came bounding out of the trees and ran straight toward Millie. Thankfully, it didn't hit her dead on but just clipped her. Which was bad enough, sending Millie to the ground."

George was furious. "What directions did it go? Whose dog was it?" He was ready for a reckoning with the dog's owners.

"Honey, for now can you just get the cart? I don't think I'm up to hopping home." She smiled weakly, her eyes wet as tears pooled in them and dribbled down the side of her face.

"I can carry you Sweets."

"Oh George-boy, no you can't. Please, go get the cart."

"I'll stay with her, George." I offered.

George surveyed the two of us and the surrounding area to make sure the dog truly had left.

"Okay. I'll be back in a jiff."

"George, honey, bring me my pain pills and some water too, please."

"Sure, thing Sweets. Be right back." He turned trotting to the office faster than I'd expect from an older guy.

After George left, Millie asked me to help her sit up. As my adrenaline started to subside, I began chattering in a nervous non-stop manner.

"Gosh that was scary. I saw a mass of black fur just about pummeled you. When I saw you slam down onto the ground and heard you scream, I knew he had broken every bone in your body. Then I saw your leg all twisted. God, I almost wretched." I heard what I had just said, "Oh, sorry. Sorry, I didn't mean that."

"No...no...don't worry. I did wretch the first few times I saw the thing and had to learn how to put it on...and walk with it."

"I thought you were broken into a thousand pieces." I caught myself again and tried to change the image of Millie twisted and writhing on the ground. "I've actually worked with one or two people who have artificial limps in physical therapy. I always loved to help them learn just how much they could do once they got comfortable with their prothesis."

Millie nodded, "It's pretty realistic but it sure felt strange at first. I'm used to it now."

"How'd it happen? Oh, sorry, none of my business."

"It was cancer. A rare cancer in my leg. I was diagnosed ten years ago this past December. Worst holiday in my life. I should have been singing carols and baking up a storm with all the kids and grandbabies around like we usually did. Instead, I had to wait through Christmas for answers. Baking just didn't have that holiday feel about it. The only thing rising in our house was fear sprinkled with tears and sugary words of hope no one could swallow."

"That must have been horrible."

"I knew I was dying. We all felt it. I fully believed that the doctor would give me just weeks to live or something like that. I was trying to be strong for the family; I mean it was Christmas. I had the grandkids singing happy birthday to Jesus and I am crying like a baby. Real strong right? My kids weren't much better at faking it either."

"I would have hidden under my comforter." I said, remembering that I had done exactly that for many, many months.

"Believe me I wanted to, but George was such a support. He was a real gem; kept me grounded. He told me, don't let your mind run off like that Millie, don't court trouble. He actually made Christmas morning joyful. That man. I am forever grateful."

Millie breathed deeply and let it out slowly willing the pain to exit her aching limb. "And he was right. I finally found out that I wasn't dying. Everything they tried to do, surgery, chemo, radiation, none of it helped. The cancer was pretty aggressive. After three months of treatment without results we had to talk about amputating. Repulsive as that sounded at the time, it saved my life. Ten years worth and counting."

Millie shook her head, "Oh but you don't want to hear all this. We've all got our troubles. We all have to face our pains and sorrows. Life throws punches at everyone's gut, eventually. Why should I be any different?"

Millie saw the cloud of sorrow come over my face. It wasn't empathy at hearing Millie's story, it was personal. "Oh, dear me. I've upset you."

"No..." I choked, "No... it's...no..." I lowered my head and tried unsuccessfully not to cry. Thankfully I heard the cart as George called out, "Your carriage awaits you." He eased out of the cart, a bottle of water in one hand, pills in the other.

I got up, "I've gotta go." I patted Millie's shoulder and hastily walked off past George.

"Thanks." He called out to my back.

"What was that about? She always seems to bolt when I'm around. Is it me?" He asked as he got to Millie handing her the water and pills.

"No. No. It was something I said, I think. It's not you dear; you're a teddy bear. That's a hurting girl there, for sure."

"Well, I am here for my hurting girl. Come on Sweets let me get you into the cart."

After swallowing a large chug of water Millie whispered, "Could you let me lay here until the pain starts to lessen?"

"Oh sure, better idea, much better idea." George sat down beside the love of his life and draped his arm over her shoulder drawing Molly gently to him. The reassuring cuddle soothed Millie as she waited for the meds to kick in.

CHAPTER TWENTY

After

THE FALL

I headed back to my van breathing in, then out as the adrenaline seeped from my body. I couldn't pace in the camper – it was too small – or I would have. Instead, Peaches was doing it for me, picking up on my nervous state of mind. Next thing I knew, I had dialed my brother Danny as tears escaped from my eyes.

"Janine, you don't sound too good. What's going on?" His sensitivity made me cry harder.

"...running... her leg..."

"Catch your breath sis, talk to me. What happened? Are you okay?"

"Millie. Her leg fell off. This dumb dog slammed into her. It was horrible. It was my fault. I did it. Oh, how could I. So horrible..." I was crying and couldn't catch my breath.

"Her leg fell off, sis? What are you talking about?" He paused, quieted his tone and spoke again. "I want to hear this, tell me what happened. I'm listening." He asked this in a slow calming voice, the voice that encourages people in counseling to unburden their souls. His mind was racing with thoughts of Janine witnessing another crumbled body.

"I'm at a campground." I could finally say. My brother's voice was helping me regain some composure.

"Ok...good...good...there's more. What happened then?"

I paused then explained, "I was out jogging and the lady who runs the place got knocked over by this seventy, eighty-pound dog. She was screaming in pain. Her leg was all twisted. It was awful."

"You saw it happen. Oh Janine, that is very upsetting."

"Yes. I was jogging and the dog came at me. I waved my arms and shouted at it to go home. It worked, but it went right at her. I shooed it right toward her!! It knocked her down and her leg was bent all crooked like."

"Oh, sis that must have been awful. Just awful."

"Turns out, it was a fake leg. I guess it twisted and, I don't know, but it was a mess and she was really hurting. It's all my fault. I should have just grabbed onto the dog and led it home or something. That poor lady. She was so nice to me when I checked in earlier." I sobbed, "It's on me Danny. That poor woman."

"Janine..." Danny spoke softly.

She sucked in a deep breath. "Uh huh?"

"Let's step back a minute and look at what happened. You can't take all this on as your doing. How did *you* cause this to happen?"

Exasperated, I snapped, "I scared the dog and it ran at her full force, knocking her over. When will I get it right? When will I stop getting people hurt!!"

"Oh sis...that's isn't so. Come on. You were jogging. We all know how to respond when there's a threat by a stray animal, a dog. We know how to react to minimize getting injured. You have to react quickly to minimize the potential threat. After all these years of running it's automatic. Isn't that what you did by instantly shooing the dog away?"

"Yes but...but...I spooked the dog and it rammed into Millie."

"Did you let it out without a leash?"

Shaking her head she responded. "Huh? What? No."

"So, you just defended yourself. Standard protocol."

"Well, if you put it that way." They were quiet, Danny letting his sister absorb the truth.

To test the waters he asked, "Who's the responsible party here or the irresponsible party? You?"

"No Danny, not me. The dog's owners." The tension left my body as I absorbed Danny's words.

"That still doesn't take away how disturbing it is to see someone get hurt. Especially an older person knocked hard to the ground. That unsettling. That's enough to deal with. No need to take on a burden that isn't yours."

"I took off the fake leg and that helped ease the pain. Thankfully her husband came, then he went to get a golf cart to take her home. "

Danny went into story mode, "Remember my buddy, Greg, you know him, with the hook for a hand; the musician. He can play any instrument. I remember when I first met him, I wanted to ask him twenty questions about what happened and how with his hook he could do almost anything."

"That was my big mistake. I did ask Millie. She had to have her leg amputated to stop cancer. Oh Danny, she said everyone has their troubles." I sniffed holding back a tear, "She doesn't even know about me, but it was like she did know. Like she was speaking to me. She only lost a leg; I lost so much more. If I had been watching Casey more closely. If I had gone outside with her."

I became distraught again, sobbing loudly into the phone. Peaches began pacing again, up on the bed, then back down and around our tiny camper.

My pain became irrational with anger, striking out, "And besides, she's old. Things are supposed to happen when you get old. You lose your sense of balance, are less steady and trip easily on uneven surfaces. You can expect accidents, right? I mean, Ken and I were young. We had our whole lives ahead of us. Casey was a child! A CHILD! It wasn't fair!"

"Losing Casey is beyond painful. To never hear her giggle again or hold her this side of heaven. I get it." He paused, waiting to see if I would respond. When I didn't, Danny continued. "Janine...sis, I am sure this lady wasn't trying to make light of your life. Ya know, I bet she has cried heart-wrenching tears just like you. Like we all have when tragedy strikes. Pain is pain sis. It's searing and it burns deeply no matter what sets it off. No matter how old you are."

"Oh, Danny you don't even know. You don't know!" I cried into the phone.

"Yes, sis, I do know. I do. Mom and Dad do. Aunt Sally does. Even Ken. Especially Ken."

That got my attention. I felt self-absorbed. Rarely had I considered the heartache of others as I hid away from my own feelings.

Sensing where Janine's thoughts had gone, Danny assured her, "It's hard to control intense emotions that are unleashed by a devastating loss. I also think you're starting to come out of it. You are beginning to move outside of yourself, to see beyond just trying to survive your pain. You're healing Janine. This is good."

We each sat quietly holding their phones listening as the truth settled in. Then movement caught my eye. "Oh no, poor Peaches is pacing like mad. I think she has to piddle."

"Piddle Peaches?" I asked, which made Peaches pace even faster and she threw in a yap to make sure I got the message.

I thanked Danny and we said goodbye, hanging up just in time. Peaches ran out the door before it was barely open. I left Peaches outside and went to place my cell in its designated place. I noticed there were messages. *"Darn. I had it on silent."* I didn't listen to the messages but checked caller ID, figuring the callers, my parents and my aunt, were just checking up on me. I shot off a quick text, "am fine - WC in a few days - luv you" and put the phone in the cup holder on my dash.

When Peaches returned, she looked right into my eyes and gave me what-for. *"Girl, you know when nature calls, I've got to answer. No more of this hangin' on the phone and ignoring me!"*

"Oh, sorry Peaches. Did I neglect you? Come, sit with me while I read. We all have our sorrows to bear, little girl, we all have our sorrows." That was a statement I would always remember. We all have our sorrows.

Before opening the latest Parker novel, a traveling gift to myself, I sat in the feeling of release that came from having seen inside myself. It wasn't pretty. I had been so pitiful for too long, but that was being tempered by a new understanding and a better sense of self-compassion and relief. And the ability to see how others were hurt by life's tragedies. *I'm ready to live again. I want to live. Mostly, I want to see beyond myself.*

I thought about my ex-husband Ken. Daddy's little girl was taken from him in a flash.

I didn't like that I had discounted everyone else's grief in light of my own. But I accepted Danny's explanation about the effect of intense grief. That was then. This was now. I would be more aware of others. I turned to the window, gazed up at the not-quite-darkened sky and said out loud, "Thank you."

Peaches responded, "You mean me."

"Oh Peaches, no more self-absorption for me, little lady." I petted her soft silky hair.

"Well, that's good to hear. I can use a little more pampering. Oooh, could you rub my belly?" Peaches stretched out and rolled over to make sure I got the message.

CHAPTER TWENTY-ONE

When Life

WAS GOOD

I grew up in Langley, a small town on the southern coast of Whidbey Island in the Puget Sound north of Seattle, Washington. Known for its extraordinarily artistic residents, the eclectically diverse community was home to mainstream artist, dabblers, old-time hippies and any number of creatively passionate people. With more such people coming and going throughout the tourist season. I didn't have an artsy bone in my lean body. I was a sports nut. If I could run, jump, ride or dribble I was happy.

My horizons were expanded with a quick ferry ride to Mukilteo, on the mainland, and on to Seattle with all that a city could offer; Pike's Place Market, the theatre, shopping, walking around Pioneer Square, the Space Needle and the best attraction for me...sports, live and up close.

As a kid, along with my dad and Danny, we had watched the final game played at the Kingdome between the Mariner's and the Texas Rangers. My dad often called me "the kid" just like the nickname for Ken Griffey Jr. It was at that game where Junior hit a 3-run homerun. He helped the Mariner's beat Texas 5-2. A few years later we returned to watch the Kingdome be imploded, marking the end of an era. The acceptance of

Safeco Field was made easier because we had box seats to the first game the Mariner's played there.

At least twice year I went to Key Arena, again box seats [it pays to have a mayor for your dad] to watch the Sonics. I had a crush on Luke Ridnour, a Washington state boy, whose rise in basketball I witnessed firsthand, having watched him play through his high school years. Even while Luke was in high school, I could see how gifted he was; fluid on the court. I was good at basketball, in an everyday sort of way. Mostly I just loved the pace, competition and discipline of playing sports. Whether I won or lost, was a starter or second string, I enjoyed every game I ever played, from basketball, to softball and even running track. I understood the work it took to win, which explained how I came to appreciate and recognize truly gifted athletes, like Junior and Luke.

I wasn't strong enough in any one sport to gain a scholarship but thankfully my mom made sure I gave as much to my studies as I did to sports. As it turned out I had a pretty good GPA and got a few scholarships.

True to the city-girl side of me I went to the University of Washington [U-Dub as we say] in Seattle. Well truth be told; everyone knew why I chose the UW. I wanted to stay as close to Langley or to be more specific, as close to Ken as possible. Ken and I had known each other since the day he stole my bat, stating, "Girls don't need baseball bats. Gimme that." I hated him!

Ken soon learned differently about girls and bats. At least this girl! We became baseball competitors from then on. Any sandlot game or family gathering caused an impromptu game to arise. If Ken and I were there, we'd be on opposing teams, welcoming the rivalry. As we got older and sports became far more formal, separating the boys from the girls on most teams, we began to support each other from the sidelines and by rehashing the plays after games. A habit that spurred each other on to play better.

Ken had no interest in college. His life was right there in Langley. He grew up around his dad's wood shop and retail store. He got his first job there and after high school was being groomed to take over; Ken &

Sons Forest Creations, in downtown Langley. Ken's dad, Kenny Sr., was an artist and a craftsman. He made his living and supported his family through the proceeds from his giftedness at crafting raw wood into furniture and beautifully crafted décor pieces. Senior culled wood from the entire western region and even took trips to Alaska every few years to arrange for a shipment of Sitka spruce and red alder. Sure, you could find those species in Washington but not the halibut. Senior consistently found a lofty catch of halibut following him back home after every trip north. What's a man to do?

There was no pressure for Ken to be part of the family business. It wasn't needed. Wood was as much a part of Ken as it was to his dad. He had begun helping his dad out even before he held a bat. He loved being in the shop and working with wood or out tromping through some new forest sizing up the growth and imagining what could be crafted from it.

In fact, once our friendship took hold, every bat Ken or I ever swung, when it wasn't aluminum, was made by Ken, perfectly shaped and weighted. These were more than bats; these were works of art, a talent Ken had inherited from his dad.

Ken knew exactly what he wanted to do with his life and that he wanted to do life with me. I had no hesitation when it came to spending my life with Ken, but deciding who I wanted to be when I grew up changed every semester. Gee, what happened to the planner in e that had my life all mapped out? It was the university, it offered far too many choices.

Remember my childhood goal to be a physical therapist? I don't know why but once I hit college, I went in ten different directions. I went through majors like a person with a cold goes through tissues. Grab, sniff, toss. Ecology, accounting, teaching, linguistics. Had I not graduated I would still be deciding what major to declare. There were too many exciting possibilities. *Why limit yourself*, I always said. In the end it was sports that drew me back to physical therapy.

Ken teased me unmercifully, "With your diverse education, you can now study the ancient hippie tribes of Langley while raising a brood of bi-lingual kids, coaching their baseball teams and handling the finances for the shop?"

"Don't forget making meals straight from my organic garden." I retorted.

By my last year at the UW, we were married. Ken spent several nights at my studio apartment near the UW campus. I came to his cozy two-bedroom cottage in Langley for the weekends. The days we weren't together we talked late into the night on the phone until I graduated and moved back home. I was four months pregnant but still took on my first PT job at Pro Physical Therapy. I started as an intern as I continued my pursuit to become a Doctor of Physical Therapy. I could do some of my studies online but I had to go to the UW for hands-on learning at least once a week.

In the month between finding out about our pregnancy, my graduation, and my move back to Langley, Ken had been busy. When I finally arrived home, I went to throw my duffle bag of belongings into the spare room to unpack later. I opened the spare room door and gasped.

The always-a-mess room with multi-sized, randomly stacked storage bins and boxes was spotless. The chaotic clutter had given way to a maple handcrafted crib and rocking chair.

Ken stood right behind me beaming. I gently moved my hand over every facet; the smooth railing, the intricately carved headboard, the curve of the spindles, the polished grain of the wood. I lowered my nose and took in the smell of the oiled maple. I sat in the rocker letting out a sigh at the comfort it afforded me.

Ken leaned against the wall and absorbed my joy with as much pleasure as he had experienced when crafting each piece of our child's bedroom. "There's more. I'm working on a dresser. And whatever else you think our baby needs. Just tell me, I'll make it."

My heart burst with love as I got up and crossed the room to Ken. "Hmm...well there is one thing." I said, with a mischievous smile.

He smiled back, eyes laughing. "Look in the closet." He told me.

My eyebrows shot up, questioning. I went to the closet, tiny as it was, opened it and let out a squeal, then turned back to face Ken, a pint-sized baseball bat in hand. "You read my mind."

"Boy or girl, that there is our first child's first bat. We'll be there for every game." The pride of fatherhood packed into each word.

I could not contain my joy. I placed the bat in the crib, ran to Ken, jumped into his arms and smothered him with kisses. I was home, home to stay and we were having a baby!

Da. Da.

What baby? Da?

Daaa.

Oooo... Casey, say Daddy. Daddy.

Da. Da.

I'm dialing with one hand as I smile with

pride at the first words out of Casey.

Ken answers. We're on speaker.

"Listen to this Ken. Say Daddy."

Da. Dada.

"DaDa. That's me!" Ken says with pride.

They DaDa'd back and forth until

a customer came into the shop

and Ken said good bye.

I turned to Casey.

Say momma. Momma.

Daaaa Da.

Chapter Twenty-Three

Spring

is Coming

Winter was giving way to spring as the weather turned neurotic. Rainy and cold one day then bright sunshine hinting of days to come, the next. Just as people relegated their puffer coats to the back of the closet, the weather would decide to be winter again. Even knowing this would happen, most resident in the Pacific Northwest tried to drag spring into being by ditching their bulky winter gear. At the hint of spring, out came the shorts, sandals [with socks] and a light hooded jacket. Hoods were a way of life because rain was a way of life. Whether a sprinkle or a deluge, Washingtonians were ready.

Though Ken couldn't see Danny on the coast he could picture him jumping from the side of the boat onto the dock just as Otis Redding started crooning *"Sittin' by the Dock of the Bay"*. That was Danny's ringtone, a classic, before their time. When Ken had uploaded it onto Danny's phone, years ago, it became a keeper. Danny sung right along with his phone each time it rang.

It was a chilly March day as Danny slipped off his thick gloves and fumbling, dug down deep into the pockets of his heavy yellow slicker. He smiled when he saw who was calling and answered, "Hello Ken."

"Hey Danny."

"Bro." Danny was tying off his boat as they spoke. Ken heard him huff as Danny tightened the line to secure the boat. "Ok my boat's secure. What's up?"

"Seems like just last weekend you were fighting the waves trying to get back into shore on that rugged coast of yours."

Danny laughed, "That sure wasn't me man! The waves calm at my command."

"Sure-thing *Father* Dan!"

Ken and Danny could not have been more opposite. Yet growing up together and having Janine in common, they forged a lasting friendship. Danny didn't have the athletic build or the ambition that came naturally to his sister or Ken, both three years older than Danny.

Ken was a muscular fit guy well above six feet, whereas Danny came in as the runt of the litter at 5'8" with the every-man's build. He loved fishing boats and the people who made their living with them, which drew him to the rugged Oregon coast's weather. He now lived there and served in a local church. He wasn't a true fisherman, truth be told. He tended to be a fair-weather outdoorsman. Further contrast between the two friends was their chosen activities; Danny preferred a good game on TV than actually playing a sport. Ken, like Janine, was always on one playing field or another. At times they were able to convince Danny to join. Surprisingly, he was pretty good. Still, sports wasn't his thing.

Just like the rhythm of the seas, the ebb and flow, Ken rolled in with a call every few months. Initially it had been out of desperation, bearing his decimated soul knowing that Danny, as a priest and friend, would be there for him and would understand. Danny was encouraged when the calls became just touching base and not totally the outpouring of grief.

Ken wasn't good at small talk and was quick to speak what was pressing on him, unless he was hesitant about how to broach a subject. Then he chattered like he was doing on this call. After a few minutes Ken paused.

"Danny, it's spring."

"I know man. Your birthday is coming and just after that, Casey's birthday."

"Mom and Dad want to celebrate my birthday, something simple, ya know, a family thing. I don't know what they want to do. It just doesn't feel right. The two most important people to me would be missing, Janine and our precious Casey."

"Janine." Danny uttered softly; the name holds its own kind of loss.

Ken didn't answer, he just sighed. The silence settled.

Ken spoke softly, "I ought to call my aunt, see if Janine will talk to me; see how she's doing. Ya think? What should I do Danny, should I call her? Do you think Janine is ready to talk? You know I want her back. You know I can't stand living without her. Not having Casey is bad, really bad. But not having Jani is the worst."

"I know how much you love her, Ken. But Janine made herself very clear when she served you with divorce papers. You can't put your life on hold waiting, hoping. Like we've talked about before. It's probably best to give her space. If she wants to reconnect, I'm sure you will get a call from her. Just keep living your life, Ken. And keep praying."

It was encouraging to hear that Ken hadn't totally stopped living. Not like Janine. Yes, he grieved, and his life stalled. He had felt such pain that he thought he could never recover. He waded through powerful emotions that pinned him to that rough-edged wall of sorrow. Tortuous splinters stabbed at him with no salve that could calm the ripping apart of his body and soul. Emotions he had never known existed, intruded into what had been his ideal life. Slowly, the force that had held him immobile lessened to a point that he could contain it, regain his balance, and continue on, lethargically at times. Several months after receiving the divorce papers, he even tried to date, at his sister's urging. That just didn't feel right. He gave himself credit, at least he had tried. The unsigned divorce papers were further proof that dating was not for him. No matter what good intended encouragement he got from others, to him there was no one that could replace Janine.

Instead of the dating scene, he drew upon the same determination he used when playing sports. He chose to live life as normally as possible. He knew he had changed, that he had a new normal which included bouts of heartache. But he also knew his life was not over, just different, very, very different. The sorrow had hit him like a tsunami, the wave crashing down, almost crushing him, drowning him, scraping him along the ocean floor. Eventually, miraculously, his feet had found solid ground, he forced himself out and up, gasping for air. He was still tentative but he was moving, breathing, rebuilding.

There were only a handful of days on his internal calendar that brought up memories; that could pull him down under again like an emotional tidal wave.

Continuing his phone call to Danny, he responded, "You're right Danny. I guess I just needed you to remind me. I'll give Janine space and keep hoping, praying."

"Look Ken, you and Janine were dumped on with more than your share of sorrow, as far I am concerned. Hard stuff, but you have gotten through it, gotten your feet back under you. You're resilient, you can get through June."

"Maybe." Ken said reluctantly, "Will you do something for me?"

"Anything bro."

"When you hear from Janine, let me know how she's doing. Just so I know. I promise not to intrude. I'll wait for her to contact me."

"Sure, Ken I can do that.

They talked about the shop, how the improving economy was bringing life back to Langley tourism. Ken explained the business was doing ever since his brother Rob had left to teaching at the local high school.

"Has your dad finally retired?"

"Semi. He always loves to putter in the shop a few times a week. He uses the retirement excuse to leave the bookkeeping to us! Get this. He's going to help a guy sail his boat down to Catalina Island in California and maybe further, depending on how it goes."

"Now that will be an adventure. Tell him to swing in for a visit with me if time allows.

"For sure."

Speaking of trying something new, have you ever thought of crafting something in wood to honor Casey for her birthday?"

"No, I haven't. Good idea Danny. I'll give that some thought. Well, I guess I'd better get back to it. Our men's softball league begins playoffs this weekend. Say a little prayer for our team, Father."

"You know I will. I've seen you swing a bat!"

CHAPTER TWENTY-FOUR

Expecting

BAD NEWS

Finally spring had fully arrived. May meant the rhododendron were in full bloom. Ken was in the shop creating a custom cherry bedroom set for a customer when the phone rang. It was from Danny, his brother-in-law who he hadn't heard from since March. Somehow he knew it was the call his heart had been subconsciously waiting for all these months. With trepidation, he sensed this call would be more than checking in. Danny had news. He felt it in my bones. Bad news. The kind of news he did not want to hear.

"Hey Ken, how's it going man?"

Ken liked Danny. He was always fun, had a warped sense of humor and for a time there, he was big into practical jokes. They've had a lifelong friendship since growing up in a small town on an island. He became a priest! Shocker there. Because he loved being out on the water catching whatever was in season. Ken saw Danny becoming a professional fisherman. Whenever Ken would mention that Danny would come back with, "Yup I'm a fisher of men. Very Biblical."

As a man of the clothe, he had a gift. Though the "kid" Danny was a jokester, Danny the man, the priest, had this uncanny ability to connect with people. Let the robe not fool you, he was also an astute business man after years by his father's side as the mayor of Langley. He networked, connecting with business and shop owners, joined the chamber of commerce and got involved helping with major events, often taking the lead.

It was always good to hear Danny's voice, but this was going to be bad. Ken's whole body tensed.

"Doin' pretty good Danny, how about you?" *Why doesn't he just quit with the pleasantries and tell me.*

"We just started a food drive. The two food banks are running low on supplies. While we get people to donate, we are also approaching grocery stores and restaurants to see how they can be involved. We'd like to keep a steady stream of supplies coming in, daily if possible."

Ken tamped down his exasperation, "That sounds like a good plan. Here in Langley, well your dad got the ball rolling on businesses supporting the local food bank. Having the community involved is critical to the success."

Dan was surprised that Ken remembered that, "It was what my dad did in Langley that sparked the idea. I reached out to him and he gave me a few strategies and ideas. Hopefully, it will take hold down here like it has in Langley. On another note, I have news about Janine."

Ken froze as his thoughts burst. *Here it comes. I knew what was coming; felt it for a while now. Janine and I had lost our daughter. The hole in my heart was huge. How does a heart even beat after being ripped open so widely? Then Janine had a total disintegration after Casey's death. She wanted a divorce and left Langley. The online divorce documents she had found went back and forth over the next few months and sat unsigned on my desk at home, under my Bible. The Bible we used to read together and to Casey. After losing Casey I got up every day, worked at the shop, talked to people, took orders, all of it. I did it for Casey. I did it for Janine. How would Casey's life matter if mine ended along with hers. Who would Janine find ready to be there for her when she finally was open to having me. A lifeless husband or me waiting to embrace life with her.*

After no interaction with her for far too long, Ken came to accept that Janine's life, or his, didn't matter to her. Without consciously knowing it, he had prepared himself for the worst, the call that she had completely given up, that she had finally decided it was all too much. Had she found a way to end her pain and sorrow like Ken was afraid she would do? What hurt him deeply was that his outgoing, always positive wife, had lost every ounce of hope. Now Danny was going to tell him what he did not want to hear. Ken braced himself, knowing nothing would help him through what he was about to hear.

This was that dreaded call. Danny was about to tell me it was over; Janine ended her pain permanently. He took a deep slow breath.

"I'm ready. You can tell me Danny."

"She's gone..."

Ken's gasp cut him off. "How?"

"A van... a camper van."

"Huh? What a car accident?" He wanted to hear but he didn't, stalling with questions. "You can tell me Danny. What happened? Did she get hit?"

"Wait. Whoa. Ken. Let's start again. Janine left your aunt's place in a camper van. She wasn't in an accident. She's on a trip, wanting to rebuild her life."

"She's not gone, gone?"

Danny jumped in to reassure him. "No. No bro. Not at all. The total opposite."

Still confused Ken asked, "She's in a camper van? Really. Alive? Wanting to live!!" He was ready for Janine to die. He wasn't ready for her to be alive, to want to live.

What came to mind was the first day Ken saw her many years ago, as a smart-mouth kid who thought she could best him on the ball field.

Janine always tells the story of them constantly competing during their childhood. Not true.

Ken just took his cues from her and did whatever was needed to be near her. An infatuated boy became a man in love, a father in love and still now, after everything that's happened, his love for Janine remains. Actually, it is stronger as if the strength of his love could somehow pull her back to life. Even all those nights he prepared for the worst, that she might die, Ken prayed his love would find a way to reach her.

Danny filled him in, "She's got Peaches and together they are heading to Dungeness. She says she must face where it all started to reclaim her life. She sounded tentative with an undercurrent of determination. Some of the old Janine came through."

"Dungeness. Good. Good for her. You know I went back. It helped."

Ken realized he was pacing and made himself sit down on the couch. They talked for another half hour. Some about life, but mostly the kind of chatting that allowed Danny to assess how Ken was taking the news. Father Danny, always the priest. The right guy at the right moment.

And Ken? Well he was elated. His days were a hot air balloon with a leak. It sputtered along as Ken frantically hoped the damage could be found, could be repaired, while also preparing for the crash he knew was inevitable.

They didn't crash. Janine didn't let death take her. The balloon was patched and Ken was soaring, shouting to the wispy cloud in the distance. *We're alive. We're alive.*

Even if he never sees Janine again, Janine had chosen to live. Ok, that sentence about even *if he never sees Janine again*. Not true. Ken yearn to see her. He ached to hold her. He prayed unceasingly that one day it would happen.

Janine is alive!

Hope abounds.

Sitting in church, a smidgin' wiggly.
Casey declares,
"I used to see Jesus in church. He's gone now.
Pastor David is gone too."
Daddy, "They are together little one.
Both are in Heaven."
Casey, "Jesus lives in Heaven and
in our hearts, Daddy."
"Yes Casey," tapping his heart,
"Jesus is right here."

CHAPTER TWENTY-SIX

Challenge

ACCEPTED

Peaches woke up, stretched her tiny legs, and then sat by my head with her tail wagging, ready to welcome the new day. I didn't open my eyes. In fact, Peaches realized, I was snoring, that grumbling, humming noise that usually calms Peaches when she was restless.

Since Peaches understood that the best part about being a dog was those nice long snoozes, she curled back up against the curve of my neck and returned to sleep. Her only thought, *no need to rush into the day.*

An hour later I opened my eyes, wiggled my toes and was starting to turn over onto my back when I felt the warmth of Peaches' feathery light-weight snuggled into the crook of my neck. "Gee, one of these days I might crush you little girl," I said as I nudge Peaches aside.

"Oh, you're finally awake." Peaches said, her snout right in my face as she gave me a kiss. *"Good morning sunshine. How about you open the door for me?"* She announced with a kitten's mew. Wait you're a dog, you don't mew. *"Mew. Mew. I'm bilingual."*

Even with her mewing, I wasn't ready to have my feet hit the ground. When I glanced over to the kitchen area, the clock announced that morning was well under way. That meant Peaches could not be delayed. I scooped up my tiny "kitten", shuffled to the van door, carried Peaches down the step, and then returned to make coffee while Peaches – well you know.

With coffee in hand, an oversized mug, I went out to join Peaches and enjoy the warm morning sunshine; the checklist in my mind coming to life. Top on my list was to inquire about Millie, which led to the thought of staying around another day or two. I still remembered Millie's initial greeting, that I could always stay longer if I wanted.

If I was staying, then I'd take the bike off the back of the van and go for a ride on that trail at the other end of the campground. Oh, and text the family to let them know I doing just fine.

Once I had mentally charted out my day, I sat back in my camp chair and enjoyed my coffee while flipping through an old magazine that had come with the van "Place to Visit in Maine." Peaches stretched out, belly up, in a patch of sun watching birds flitting through the trees. If she was truly a cat, she's be launching herself in their direction.

Two hours later, I had leisurely consumed two mugs of coffee, taken a short walk, and showered. I was back in my lounge chair texting my family.

Made good progress driving.

Nice campground ... all is good

luv J

I put Peaches in the van, which was shaded by the one tree on my site. I made sure the inside was well ventilated, then headed toward the office to see how Millie was. As I got closer, I noticed a line of motorhomes, trailers, and a van packed to the top of all its windows with a bulging cargo holder on the roof. The vehicles were lined up to register and set up camp.

I hesitantly waved at George who was escorting a family towing their pop up. He waved back as he kept up his conversation with the new campers. I entered the office to find a bustling Millie, the remnants of pain still etched on her face, trying to answer multiple questions that two different groups were asking at the same. I felt called to action; I went behind the counter, gave Millie a brief hug and located the stack of blank registration slips.

I remembered having filled one out the day before. I began passing them out to those waiting to check in, "Please fill these out, then Millie will take your money and George will be out front to escort you to your site."

Millie gave a sigh of relief as the crowd started to relax and accepted that check-in would take a little bit longer than they expected. Having a second person seemed to put people more at ease. Meanwhile, I went into the office on the other side of Millie, who had just taken payment from a young couple and was handing them a map of the campgrounds. I pulled a bar-height chair over to the counter and motioned for Millie to sit.

"Here Millie, let me do that. You collect the money."

I took the map and guided the couple to the end of the counter. "Now, let me show you where you'll be. Let's see you're in site E78. You can wait for George to escort you or, if you just go down this road here... keep in mind everything it is one way..."

I continued to go from handing out registration cards to giving people their maps and directions to their site, then letting them know that George would be happy to escort them and help in any way he could. I ended with, "Welcome to EZ Breezee." I was tempted to say, "Ya all." But refrained.

Life-long bonds can be formed from deep adversity, from the pit of battle, from staring down fear when facing an aggressor, and from helping an over-wrought Millie at the registration counter. Yup, we bonded.

"I don't think I have ever had a day like this is all our years of workkamping." Millie exclaimed when the surge finally ended. We sat slowly drinking from chilled bottles of water. She discreetly took a pill from her pocket and washed it down with a sip of water and a sigh.

I wanted to ask how she was doing but truthfully, I could see it on her face. Instead, I chatted, "I remember one summer on Whidbey Island. I don't know what spurred it on, but tourists swarmed the place like locust. Ken, now my ex, called me, desperately pleading for me to help out in his dad's store. It was a mad house of buyers and lookers. But this, here, today. Wow. Crazy!"

"You sure saved me. What a sight to see you walk behind the counter and jump in to help. Calmed everyone right down. Even me."

"Did you see that family from the van. How many kids did they have with them?"

"Oh at least fifty." Millie laughed, "All with candy coated faces and smiles of anticipation."

"But so well behaved, even with sugar in them."

Millie's laugh became boisterous. I joined in.

For a while, we compared notes on campers, laughing with the laughter of those who have survived an unprecedented onslaught. We saw George approaching the office in his cart. He took out his hanky, mopped his brow, parked the cart and made his way into the office.

"Who forecasted that downpour of people!" He called out to Millie, nodding to me. "Did you see that van...."

"...Filled with kids on sugar..." Millie and I said together, still laughing.

As he sat down next to Millie, a caring question in his eyes. Millie just smiled gently and did a slow blink.

With a sigh George proclaimed, "Man, I'm starving."

When he saw Millie begin to respond he stopped her, "No Sweets, let me get us something to eat."

I jumped up, "I'll do it. Point me in the right direction. You two have a few moments together."

From that day forward the three amigos were a team. Well, the two amigas and one amigo were a team. I stayed a week. After my morning routine, which included time with Peaches, jogging or a bike ride, I headed to the office at peak time to assist with check in for those arriving and I gave a list of departures to the couple who cleaned up the vacated sites.

Millie smiled, greeted people as they came in and after I got their paper-work done, she took their payment. Like that first day, I explained the map and sent them out to George. Millie and George always shared a late lunch together and we often connected again after dinner.

One such evening Millie asked me, "Do you play Rummikubes 3D?

"Oh yes, love it."

"Care to play a few rounds?"

George cleared his throat purposefully, "Ah hum! I wouldn't if I were you. I've been playing with Millie for years. It's because I am such a nice guy that our marriage didn't dissolve that first year." He looked at his wife and smiled, "How many games am I down Sweets. How much money do I owe you?"

"Well George let's just say, if you would pay up, I could live in luxury." She turned to me with a twinkle in her eyes, "But I could always use a little extra cash for a new yacht."

"Hmmmm. Peaches and I would like a larger rig, so you're on lady. Fair warning, I never lose." Peaches, who always joined us in the evening, chimed in, *"A diamond collar would look oh so sparkly around my neck."*

Reno kept sleeping as older dogs were prone to do. It warmed my heart when Peaches snuggled up next to him. But not tonight. She was ready for the challenge, diamonds dancing through her mind.

George chuckled, "How much can you sell that little dog for. I think you are about to taste defeat."

"Well, if that is even remotely true and I emphasize remotely, then defeat will taste better than these cookies I made." When the laughter died down, I turned serious and starred directly at Millie while mixing up the tiles in the draw-bag. "Choose well Millie."

After four well-played rounds, George was standing behind Millie massaging her shoulders encouraging her. "You're tied, Sweets. You have a reputation to uphold, and that yacht was sounding pretty good.

I glanced at my tiles and gave a knowing smirk, "I think three out d Millie massaging her shoulders, encouraging her, "You're of five is a good way to end this. Don't you Millie."

We played on; it could have gone either way. Yacht or bigger rig and a diamond collar. Millie saw that I had one tile left. A friendly growl rumbled out from her, "I'm just being welcoming."

"No Millie, you just lost." I said as I laid down the last of my tiles. "Out!"

"Uuugggghhhh," Millie groaned, flipping over her three remaining tiles. Reno lifted his head to see if Millie needed his help. Peaches was twirling and dancing. She really believed a diamond collar was in her future. Cubic zirconia?

"Well Sweets, looks like you've met your match. And it feels like I am ready to call it a day."

"Me too." I said, remembering that Peaches needed to be let out for her evening piddle especially after all this excitement. I could hear her now, *"Well, well Miss Party-time girl. Did you forget who matters in your life? Who your real friend is?"* Snort, snort.

In truth she was daydreaming about diamonds with her a one track mind. I scooped her up.

"I am sure Peaches needs some personal time. See you tomorrow. Depending on how the morning goes, I'll probably be able to help you with registration and check out. Then it will be my turn to check out."

Although both Millie and George knew I was leaving and when, I got the impression that they had hoped I would, once again, extend my time at EZ Breezee.

"Leaving!" Millie said taken aback, "How do I redeem my reputation."

"Um, I think you have to come to terms with the truth Millie. Redeeming your reputation will never happen."

Aghast, Millie smiled, "But it would be fun to try."

There was such a soft lovingness behind her words that I could only respond in kind. "Yes, it would be fun. This has all been such an ideal time. I so needed just to be normal, to do everyday things and enjoy life again. Enjoy people, wonderful people like you two. I know I haven't shared much, I still can't, but ..." I choked back the lump in my throat, "You guys have made my first steps at regaining my life much easier than I expected it to be."

Millie seemed so in tune with my state of mind. It felt like she sensed it still was not time to push. I was grateful for her restraint.

"Group hug." I said, as was my tradition at the end of our evenings together. This time there was a deeper tenderness to my words.

When peaches squirmed at the center of our grouping, we stepped back. "I'll see you in the morning." Smiling from the inside out, I turned, with Peaches in my arms, to walk toward my site.

CHAPTER TWENTY-SEVEN

Royalty

When I got back to my campsite, I started to prepare for leaving EZ Breezee the next day. All the items that I would not need in the morning I put away. I got out the plastic storage bin from under my bed. I used to keep everything orderly and easy to get to when it was time to set up camp again. Or de-camp as was the case.

I unclipped the tablecloth and placed the clips in a baggie. There had been barely a breeze in this campground, but I had learned from experience that if you didn't clip down your tablecloth it could fly away to parts unknown, disrupting all food items on the table. I remembered the relish dish thrown to the ground but not before splattering the area with mayo, mustard, ketchup, pickles and onions. Try cleaning that one up. What a mess. When I saw these three-dollar metal clips at the local camping supply store I thought it was genius. I also felt liberated knowing I was not alone; others had been splattered by reality.

I wiped the dust and minor debris from the tablecloth then folded it and placed it in the bin. Each small action was connected to many memories; memories I had forced myself not to look at for so long; memories that had always been sweet but had suddenly and tragically turned bitter. I hadn't expected that folding up a tablecloth would trigger a swell of tender thoughts or the few tears I felt welling up at the pleasant memories.

"Mommy, this one. I love this one!"

"Oh yes...yes, this is the one. What do you like about it Peanut?"

Casey was my daughter's given name, but this little person necessitated a more descriptive moniker.

"It's bright with so many colors, Mommy."

"Yes, it is. Do you want to carry it?" I said as I carefully pulled a loud splashy vinyl tablecloth from the tightly packed stack on the shelf of the camping supply store.

"Can I?" My 3-year-old exclaimed as she reached out her delicate arms to be filled with the bright crinkling package. She danced it in front of herself then hugged it to her chest.

We meandered toward the checkout counter, Peanut maneuvering the packaged tablecloth which threatened to consume her as she walked in her 2" high flip flops. No, the precarious looking footwear was not my choice; like I had a choice. She may have been tiny but she was also born a princess with determination.

Somehow, I had given birth to a girly-girl, the antithesis to all that I was. From day one, this tiny parcel of love was also an adamant stubborn fashion diva. The first indication was at her birth when she scrunched up tiny, little newborn face. She greeted me with a protest to the birthing process. To add to her displeasure, Casey was indignant at how she was wrapped up in a generically pink fleece with an equally bland beany place on her head. Not the fashion statement she wanted to make upon her entry into the world. Where were the bows, the frills, the cuteness factor? Who wouldn't scrunch up their face being forced to wear such non-descript, atrocious wrappings?

I was busy packing and reminiscing when Peaches yipped to remind me that she wanted another evening walk. *"I didn't yip, that was a deep guttural bark, thank you! And you noticed, so it worked."*

I came back to the present, "I hear ya..." I said looking at Peaches whose tiny head peered out the open passenger window. "Just give me a minute."

Peaches yipped her acknowledgment. *Again, let me remind you, that was a bark. And I am feeling a bit put out right about now.*

I finished packing up everything except the lawn chair. I had gotten into the routine of welcoming the day sitting there with my coffee and thoughts. The next morning, before leaving, I would do so again; a little quiet time before hitting the road.

As I attached the leash to Peaches' multi-colored floral collar, I laughed out loud, making Peaches jump. "Oh...oh...look at you, just like princess Casey, all flower and bright colors."

Peaches recovered from her startled moment, shook her tiny body and allowed me to lift her out of the van and place her on the ground, where she primly began to lead me on her walk.

"Oh yes, Peaches you too are a princess, look at that walk."

"This is not a walk; this is royalty in motion. A queen." Peaches held her head higher, lifting her teeny tiny legs with grace and precision, sashaying along the rugged path. *"There should be a red carpeting on this path."*

To let the whole world know how poorly she was being treated by being forced to walk on the bare, unkempt ground, she sniffed in disdain. *"Yes, this time I sniffed. It was not a bark."*

It sounded like a sneeze to me. "Bless you Peaches" I said, giggling at the silly creature, more like a pile of fluff, walking along like she ruled the universe.

"You know I rule... girl!" Prance... prance...sniff...prance...prance. *"The queen is in court."*

The memory of Casey choosing that colorful tablecloth had not hurt my heart. The memory did not stab at me or draw blood. Oh my. It had actually bathed my heart in warmth. I slept soundly that night and woke up early, much earlier than I usually did, not that I had kept close track of time. I lay in bed wondering whether or not I should get up or try to go back to sleep. I decided I really was wide awake. My senses responded by craving a nice cup of coffee. That first sip of the day was always the best.

Peaches partially opened one eye, understood that I was insane to be up so early, curled up into a tight ball of fur, and disappeared into the bedding. I learned long ago to check under blankets and throws before plopping down on a bed, chair or couch. You never knew if Peaches was squirreled away unseen.

When I left Mesa, I had packed a journal in my van to enter quick daily updates about my trip. This was yet another habit from past trips. The journal remained tucked away, the pages blank as a new day. I reached into the passenger door compartment, pulled out the journal with a pen clipped to its front, grabbed my super-sized mug of coffee and headed out to my chair. A few harmonious notes of soft morning light began to play. The full orchestra underscored the day ahead.

CHAPTER TWENTY-EIGHT

My Journal

I turned to the first page of my journal and began to write...

What is this I have been feeling. It feels oddly out of place. Joy. A sense of belonging. Is this what life feels like? It has been so long, everything inside of me has been dead. Am I coming alive? Will this stay or be taken away?

I want to pray, though I haven't prayed much in quite a while. I want to thank you God but how do I do that when I still have so many questions, feelings, fears? When I still don't know what more might be taken from me.

No...no. I am not going to think about that. I want to just be. I want to sit here with this sense of belonging that is dusted with a sprinkling of joy. I had a memory of Casey and I felt joy. I felt how wonderfully loving my baby was. Seeing the joy on her face was like my first bite of softened creamy rocky-road ice cream knowing the deliciousness would multiply. My joy tripled around Casey. I could taste it.

I guess I can say thank you God for Millie and George. Their laughter, their kindness. How they both go through each day as if it were a gift. I guess it is a gift, isn't it? Maybe. I hope so anyway.

Millie and George helped me get back into living. It's feeling pretty good right now. This being-alive stoked my senses like the smells of spring that used to make me want to go camping. An undeniable pull I couldn't resist. Feeling good is mending my bruised heart.

I am saying goodbye to new friends and heading north. I think I'll drive about 400-500 miles before I start looking for a place to stop. Or maybe not.

Look Mommy. I'm swinging.
I saw Casey's chubby little fingers gripping the bat.
It's almost as big as my precious child.
Ken coaching her,
"Yay Casey, give us a home run, just like last time."
"Ken, she's only three."
"I know, right. Can you imagine her at five."
"Swing batter." Casey shouts hitting the T-ball.
She threw the bat down; it nearly took her arm with it.
Casey ran full throttle, toward Peaches [first base],
which moved at times,
then to the camp-chair [second base] and
on toward third base [a potted plant].
Spinning her legs faster and faster
she arrived back by us [home base].
Casey shakes her whole-body dancing and cheering...
"Home Run! Home Run!"

CHAPTER THIRTY

My Child,

My Child

I finished the first entry in my journal. The very first entry of my fresh start. The flow of pen across paper moved easily as my thoughts and feelings cascaded onto the blank journal page. It felt liberating. Cathartic. I gently closed the journal, holding my hand on its cover and sat in a moment of silent gratefulness.

It was still early at EZ Breezee. The air smelled fresh, moist but in a refreshing way. Rather than waiting around or waking up Millie and George, I decided to write them a little note and leave early. At times, I found I could express my true feelings much better in writing than when speaking. I wanted Millie and George to know how much they had done for me. Carefully taking out the back page from my journal, which looked like stationary with its simple embellishments, I wrote my note and included my email and phone number. These were people I wanted to stay connected to; they were not pass-through people.

I quietly folded up my camp chair, bungeed it to the back of the van, then secured my bike on the rack over the chair, put on my work gloves wrinkling my nose as I unhooked the water, sewer, and the electricity.

Phew, nothing overflowed. With the hatch battened down, I did one last check. I took off my gloves and thought, "Done…ready to go."

Grabbing my coffee cup, journal and the note, I went into the van, poured the remainder of my coffee into a travel mug and secured everything inside the van. I looked toward the unmade bed where Peaches laid still sound asleep. She wouldn't need a walk for a few hours, I'll just leave the bed as is.

I used a sanitizing wipe to clean my hands, got out my keys, and said a silent goodbye as I pulled out of the camp site. Full sunlight announced the new day. Driving slowly and as quietly as possible on a gravel packed road that none-the-less noisily crunched under my tires, I made my way toward the exit that came around behind the office, passing Millie and George's humble abode.

Sitting in a camp chair reading was Millie, who looked up at the sound of my approaching vehicle. With a wave, she beckoned me.

I pulled over and stopped, realizing that I was glad to have the chance to say goodbye in person.

"Sneaking out without paying the bill in the dead of night, are you?" Millie said just above a whisper so as not to awaken sleeping guests.

"You caught me." I replied with the soft voice of a mother trying to get her infant back to sleep. "I didn't think you would be up this early." I handed Millie the note, "I was going to leave this for you and George. Seeing you is better."

"Where are you headed?"

"Since I woke up so early, I thought I would try to go four or five hundred miles and see where that brings me." I held up my cell phone.

"Oh, that's right you have that fancy contraption that tells you where you are and how to get to where you are going."

"I left you my cell number, in the note, so we can keep in touch." I said with a hint of sadness. It never dawned on me how difficult it would be to leave. Camping is where joy came to visit me, maybe it would stay a while. It was a freshness that lightened my heart.

"What is it dear? I don't want to pry, but you know I will listen."

I didn't realize how much I needed to talk and the ideal person to talk with was right there, with kindness and compassion written on every line of her face. I sat down in the camp chair facing Millie, but I could not speak. Behind us, the mountain range still had specks of snow on the highest peaks. The park was quiet as most campers were still in dreamland. Even the dogs slept.

Millie reached over and took my hands in her own, "How 'bout we start with a prayer."

I didn't know how to respond. Only this morning I had dusted off my praying abilities. I simply lowered my head and waited.

Millie began, her voice a low rhythmic sound that felt like she sat in the presence of angels.

"Oh, Heavenly Father, who sits on high yet gazes, with love and delight, on your daughters. We are your children, and I lift up your child Janine up to you this morning."

As Millie continued, I no longer heard the words that Millie was praying. The words had become a silky gentle refrain, a hymn of tones what tied us to the heavens. I heard myself thinking, *My child. My child.*

Were those my thoughts? No. The words were being spoken into my soul, into my inner most being as if God was connecting with me. The words bringing forth a memory.

The image entered my mind. I was sitting in the rocker Ken had made for our nursery. In the middle of the night five-month-old Casey was fussing and uncomfortable. I hummed, made soothing sounds and spoke quietly. "It's ok Casey. It's ok, my child, My dear, dear child."

I wanted the overpowering love I felt for her to seep into her little being and calm her. I wanted my love to bring tranquility to her, to allow her to descend back into sleep.

With the background of Millie's rhythmic tones God was doing the same, speaking to me, *"My child. My child."*

His love wrapped around my wounds, my scars, the pain no one else had touched. He saturated me with love. It permeated my consciousness. His powerful love quieted my raging anguish, like a down jacket on a bitter winter day. Warmth. Protection. Security. Love.

I didn't know that I was speaking out loud, repeating the words of solace I was hearing, *"My child. My child."*

Then came the tears, up from the crevices of my soul crying out for release, for healing. I was not afraid; I did not try to stop what was happening. I could not; something profoundly intimate and spiritual was affecting my soul.

My child. My child

To survive, I had stuffed my intense emotions down, buried them in the grave along with my child. I would not, could not acknowledge them, afraid that the depth of my sorrow would bury me as well.

Until now.

"Blessed are those that mourn, for they shall be comforted."

I got it. The unrestrained weeping from my soul opened me up to God's voice, healing the raw edges of my wretched despair. I was being comforted.

My sobs began to quiet. I had a sense of being unshackled. The only other sounds were those of morning awakening. Millie was no longer praying out loud, though her hands were still lightly covering mine. I opened my eyes and slowly lifted my head. Millie's eyes remained closed, her head down, her lips were moving in silent prayer.

She must have felt me stir. She opened her eyes and gave a tender pat to my hands.

Without thought, the words started as I voiced my story for the first time.

I told Millie how I had married my childhood sweetheart Ken about a year before I graduated from the University of Washington. Our first few months of marriage were long distance except on weekends when either I would go back to Langley or Ken would come to Seattle. The best times were when we took in a Mariner's game. How we had planned on waiting a few years before starting a family but I had gotten pregnant in our first month of marriage. I graduated just in time to move back to Langley, settle in and give birth to Casey.

I told Millie about the surprise Ken had for me. Waiting in the nursery was furniture and the baseball bat he had made. "We named her Casey. You know, Casey at the bat. Corny I know, but we both loved the name the minute we hit on it. Um, no pun intended." Millie rolled her eyes and chuckled.

I spoke with lightheartedness about our years as a young family including our many camping trips. "One of our favorite places to camp was Dungeness Spit on the Olympic Peninsula. It was a two-hour drive. Well, depending on the ferry which we caught at Fort Casey."

I paused trying to decide if I wanted to go on; or even if I could continue. The quiet morning began to awaken with more birds chirping happily as they greeted the new day. Distant sounds of camper doors opening and closing joined in as people emerged from their rigs.

Millie just sat comfortably giving me all the time I needed.

"The Spit. Um, the last time we were at Dungeness Spit camping, just the three of us. An annual tradition. We had graduated from tenting to a small trailer."

I hesitated; I did not want to remember the details. I had been fighting to keep the details obscured from my memory. I had refused to allow my thoughts to go there. In truth, my mind had simply shut down that part of my memory and I never tried to open the door. Like the outside double door in the ground that led to dusty, dirty, smelly, bug and vermin ladened basement. Better to throw on a padlock, ignore it, walk away and don't look back.

With Millie by my side, I realized that I no longer felt shut down, no longer felt the need to hide. *"My child. My child."*

I felt safe and ready to start opening what had been locked up inside of me, eating away at my body, mind and soul.

"There was a terrible accident. A terrible... Casey." The tears began to trickle down my face. I wanted to get it all out but found myself only able to say, "Casey died."

There, I said it. The words. *Casey died.*

Two words. A proclamation that had more import than *We the people....* Somber. Heavy.

I was silent for a moment, surprised that I had not collapsed or automatically curled up inside myself to hide. I was emotionally spent but also felt freed from the reaper's hand that had gripped my heart for too long. I had wanted to say it. I needed to say it. *Casey died.*

"A few months later my marriage died too. I hid in Arizona, living with my aunt. Well, not living really. That is what this trip is about. I have to get my life back. A life, any life. I don't want to be dead anymore."

Millie was crying. Salty tears crawled down her face hovering on her chin.

We were unaware that George had gotten up, had seen us talking and quietly gone back into the kitchen. He poured coffee for himself and me, tea for Millie, then had headed for the screen door, tray in hand. He paused when he heard the tone of my voice, heard me say, Casey died. He stepped back out of sight not wanting to disrupt me as I worked to get the final words out of my broken heart.

George's heart broke as well.

I looked down. Millie leaned across the space between us and placed her hand on top of my head. "Oh, sweet Lord," Millie half spoke, half prayed, "...that is a burden too heavy for such a young woman like Janine to carry. Ken too. Oh, Father, I am profoundly sorry for all her suffering. Father, I pray mercy, grace and comfort upon your child."

I leaned into her hand and allowed this gentle woman to speak affirming words as if she knew; like she'd been there. I opened my eyes as Millie prayed softly. I saw the blanket over Millie's lap covering her legs; one leg, the other one taken by cancer. She does know suffering. Millie didn't lose a child, but she lost a part of her body. I lifted my eyes to Millie's and asked, "How did you go on Millie after...after..."

Millie tapped the book in her lap. I recognized it, her Bible. "Just this morning I was reading in Psalms. I mark up my Bible with notes and dates and comments. It turns out this morning I was reading the Psalm that helped me through some really dark times in my life."

"I haven't picked up a Bible in, well, since before..." I left the sentence unfinished, like my life.

"Would you like me to read it to you? It's about how David was in total despair. He felt abandoned by God, expressing deep anguish and despair. After pouring his heart out to Him, David remembers God's faithfulness. David is always a reminder to me that God doesn't leave us, we leave Him, while he lovingly waits for us to reach back out to Him."

Janine pauses trying to recall the verse, "That sounds familiar. Yes, please, read it."

Millie turned to Psalm 13 in her Bible and began to read.

Like David, I too began to remember God's faithfulness. Even bringing me here. I had arrived at EZ Breezee in my compact camper van, shattered but yearning to live again. I was leaving as someone else. I did not quite know who I was. I just knew I had been fed, nourished by love and God's presence and two tender-hearted people. A quiet sense of peace fluttered in my heart.

Something else happened. The constant sense of being gnawed at from the inside out, like my soul being devoured, that I had lived with all these months, had stopped. In its stead, a soothing balm of expectancy was spreading out within me. Like the orchestra from this morning had serenely reached a crescendo in surround-sound then came down softly all around my being.

George quietly walked out with a tray of coffee, tea and croissants. We sat, nibbled and sipped is silence, just being together.

The time came for me to head out. In our tradition we came together for a group hug.

CHAPTER THIRTY-ONE

Becoming

FATHER DAN

Dan was weatherly handsome, always tanned from coastal living. People gravitated to his easy manner. His open radiant smile drew people into his confidence. He could think on his feet and from his heart, exuding care and confidence when he counseled people. It was not that cocky, pound-your-chest confidence. Rather, he had an understated confidence that comes from knowing who he was and who he wasn't; from doing what he felt called to do and doing it with genuine passion. He exuded a solid, steadfastness with radiant warmth.

Dan's childhood dream was to buy and sell boats. A perfect fit for a teen drawn to the sea. It was that dream that was pushing him toward walking away from his advanced Biblical studies at Trinity Anglican University. His yearning for the ocean, the sand, and seagulls squawking overhead that never abated.

In all honesty, Dan would not have ever said that he was passionate about his faith; it was always just there, a part of him. Sure, it had been strong enough to have him choose Trinity to work for a Master of Divinity. Yet that was a choice he often didn't fully trust. At Trinity he was surrounded by fiercely dedicated future pastors and ministry leaders. That wasn't Dan. His was more of a scholarly pursuit born of curiosity. Did you need a passion to be a priest?

Dan took a hiatus from his studies when he started to become hesitant, wondering if ministry truly was for him. He was close to graduating but put his foot on the brake, jumped on a bus to Oregon, got off in Eugene then hitched a ride to the coast. He stayed there for part of the summer, becoming part of the community by volunteering every time there was an event or need. As was usually the case, he instantly became everyone's friend, the waitress, the store clerk, the kid pumping gas. He caught the eye of the police chief and mayor when he jumped in to help with the July 4th community wide celebration. They have all remained friends ever since. This all occurred during that time Janine asked if he would make it back to Whidbey to go camping with them at Dungeness Spit.

"Maybe sis, but it doesn't look likely."

"Oh Danny, it's been too long since you camped with us. Casey would love having Uncle Danny to help her collect rocks and shells."

"Hey sis, wrong denomination. Your guilt trip won't work on an Anglican." He joked. "Really, I would love to, but I am committed to Cruz the Coast days. I've been told the two-weeks of activities and endless seafood is sheer pandemonium, including fireworks on the fourth of July. I'll be back before the end of the summer and we can do some hiking, even camping then."

"Oh. yikes, if guilt doesn't work. I have no hold on you!!" Janine responded. "Except I am holding you to being back on-island before our fleeting summer passes. Casey loves you." She swooned.

"Straight to the heart. Ok you can count that as a promise sis. Text me some pictures when you're at the spit."

"Will do. Love ya Danny."

"You too sis. Hi to Ken and hug that little one for me."

They both felt that they had all the time in the world. Until a harsher reality reshaped their lives. Casey died.

That could have been when Dan left his faith, but surprisingly he was drawn to it more profoundly. The emotional impact, o Casey's death, felt like a melting snowcapped mountain that powerfully pounds downward into a river during spring. The formidable melting snow torrentially unearths trees, rocks and debris often changing the course of the river forever, a new path forged. Torrential grief changed the course of Danny's life. It ripped out all that he held as important in life leaving him to fill the void. He chose faith, returning to Trinity, this time with a new found unshakable passion.

At that point Dan knew he could not hide from faith, nor could he run from it. God was pursuing him. The more Dan gave himself to his vocation the more genuine it became. Dan learned he loved to pray; his despondent family and many others surely needed it. His scathing brokenness opened his eyes to others wounded and crushed by life. He wanted to be there for them, show them the love of Christ, His grace, mercy and comfort.

After Casey died he returned to seminary. A short time later he took his final vows. He sometimes thought he was running away. He was running from the guilt, real guilt, of not having made it home to go camping with Janine, Ken and his sweet niece Casey. He was running away from an excruciating pain that he was ill-prepared to carry alone.

True to his character, Dan was brutally honest and shared this overwhelming sense of regret with Bishop Xavier, his advisor at Trinity. Father Xavier's response astonished him at first. Dan had thought that when he acknowledged all his wrong reasons for entering the priesthood, he would be disqualified. That was not the case at all.

Bishop Xavier affirmed Dan's immense grief as the core of a good servant, "Dan, God's reason to make himself known to man is for just these times. We have a refuge under His wings. It is our hiding place and turning to your faith when the pain seems too unbearable for the soul, that is what

God wants us to do. As you let Him heal your suffering, as He walks with you out of that valley of darkness, you will gain a tremendous and very personal intimacy with your Lord and Savior and a deeper compassion for others."

"Am I hiding under His wings or running away?"

"Right now, it is the same thing Dan. God won't let you stay in hiding. He won't let you wallow and never heal if you are as open to His leading as I have come to know you to be. Lean in on Him and our Heavenly Father will bring you through with a richer and more refined faith."

Dan had accepted Bishop Xavier's words at face value. He willingly gave himself over to the counsel of his advisor and moved forward with the process of becoming a priest.

He soon realized that his prayers did not always come from his own thoughts. It seemed God was the protagonist of his prayers by placing burdens on his heart that could only be dealt with by him speaking them back to God. His prayers became a fountain of words flowing freely as he communicated with God throughout each day. He would take time to listen; his heart and soul open to the prompting of the Holy Spirit.

People drawn to Dan's amiable personality or confidence were soon taken in by his ever-present calm demeanor. Even when he was laughing, joking or teasing and cajoling, underneath the lightheartedness there was peace. His foundational understanding of the broader picture in life put people at ease and made people open themselves up, knowing Dan would listen and respond with wisdom.

When it came time to be placed in a parish Father Dan was again going to follow the advice of those who made such decisions. Wherever they assigned him he would willingly go. Bishop Xavier did not give him an assignment but gave Dan a choice; a larger parish in the suburbs or a small coastal parish. As he inhaled the remembrance of salt air into his lungs, without hesitation he chose the Oregon coast.

The retiring coastal priest, Father Harris welcomed Dan upon his arrival and hastened to get him settled in. Father Harris had served for only five years, which for him were four-years and eleven-months too long. A nice place to visit but...! Damp. Fishy smelling. Bulky tattered sweaters and worn jeans. Long hair. Nope. Father Harris yearned for refinement.

By the week's end Father Harris had given Dan the quickest summary of the parish, the workings of the parsonage and a list of administrative duties left to be done, "Oh and sort through the clothing donations weekly."

Dan thought that sorting through old clothes was about the furthest thing from ministry he could imagine. Where are the sick, the elderly, the children who need spiritual guidance, the volunteers that are the heart and soul of the church?

"Are there volunteers." Danny asked.

"Um...volunteers? Well, let's see now..." Father Harris stammered just as Melissa entered the rectory office.

"Good morning, Father Harris." She spoke softly with reserve.

"Ah...yes, Melissa." Father Harris said, then turning to Dan, "This is Father Dan. He's taking over as I move on." Before she could acknowledge Dan, Father Harris continued, "Melissa is very helpful. Yes, yes, she could be called a volunteer."

Just then the phone rang. Father Harris thought, saved by the bell. "I'll take that call in the other room. Then I'll be taking off. Godspeed." He announced and he hurried out of the community hall thinking, *Godspeed to me too, lots of speed. I'm out of here!*

Dan looked at the young woman standing before him with a baffled expression on his face. Well, young was not the correct description. She was about Danny's age, or a few years younger. Slender but not athletically built, like Janine. Feminine. She probably brought juice and snacks to whatever games her child, children played and kissed their scraped knees. Her long chestnut brown hair was pulled back into two loose braids that were held together by a plain rubber band. The misty morning air had given rise to many rebellious locks that frizzed up and sprung out all around her questioning face. Shy brown eyes averted him as Dan held out his hand in greeting, "Hi Melissa." He said softly.

He felt that anything louder than a whisper would make her bold and run. Skittish that was it. Though Melissa's eyes were not darting around the room, it seemed her whole being was. Her lips, a bit chapped from the weather, twitched, like she was trying to subdue a smile but was most likely twitching from nervousness.

She briefly took his outstretched hand letting go the moment she made contact, the color in her cheeks rising considerably "Um, welcome Father. I didn't even know Father Harris was leaving."

"Yes, he is. It seems he will be going on to a teaching position in California. I think he has family there as well."

"That's right, I remember him saying that he was from California. More accurately though, I think he couldn't wait to get away from here." At this thought she scrunched up her face as if trying to recall the exact conversation where she had heard about Father Harris's dissatisfaction with Oregon.

Seeing a multitude of expressions cross Melissa's face, Danny laughed.

Melissa went stone-still, and then smiled, "I was doing it again, right? Making faces? Aunt Eleanor always chides me on that, says I look like a giraffe chewing a mouth full of leaves!"

Unexpectedly they were both laughing. Dan felt like he was home. Melissa felt more at ease in the presence of this ruggedly handsome man. Father Harris always seem too proper and uptight. Father Dan, well, he laughed and smiled. Nice. Really nice.

They spent the next half-hour chatting about the community and Melissa's desire for the church to be more involved in the community. At first, she too had disdained clothing donations and yearned to be out helping the people that were her neighbors.

She explained, "Well, that's how I felt initially. Until I found myself praying with people or just chatting with them, making them feel loved and cared for when they were struggling. Building relationships. That's what it's about for me."

With a sudden unexpected vehemence Melissa proclaimed, "After all, Father Dan, um isn't that what church is all about. Not only what goes on inside the walls on Sundays, but what we take outside to the lives of those around us?"

"Well said Melissa. I'd say you're ready to give your first homily!"

"No way...remember, I am a mere volunteer." Her face contorted again as she tried to discern if Dan was serious. When Dan smiled, Melissa's face relaxed. "And call me Danny now that we'll be in the clothing trenches together."

Father Dan was filled with a sense of well-being, camaraderie, he had a new-found co-conspirator. Finding out Melissa was not a mother, nor was she even married, peaked Dan's interest by a few decibels, from Beethoven to AC/DC.

When he was preparing to leave Trinity Anglican University with his Masters in Divinity, he had been in such a fog that he had forgotten some teachings, seminars and counsel he had received on the pitfalls for new priests. The advice given did not hold back on any of the issues. This was brought on by the horrendous discovery of priest-pedophiles and other inappropriate relationships in the churches. Anglican priests can marry but the root problem was one of power and self-discipline. Becoming a priest in leadership warranted a course on the undue influence a priest had over parishioners. Trinity had implemented training to develop a better sense of awareness in its priests and other leaders in the church. Every person in a leadership position had an accountability partner to meet with at least monthly, That was when when they asked the tough questions and were there for open, honest discussions on any issue.

Dan was oblivious during this instruction, even as his fellow prelates laughed, joked and then finally asked each other probing questions. Dan sat on the sidelines, absorbed in sorrow, that made his peers' concerns seem trivial.

Trivial until the day he met Melissa and found himself, later that night, in his study, reliving every word that they had exchanged. He chuckled out loud at every nuance of her face, her giraffe expressions. He could not deny the feeling of the brief touch her hand had generated. He sat quietly, feeling the sensation again and again.

The moment Melissa had entered the rectory office Dan's heart had beaten a little faster. Life burst in on him catching him off guard yet craving more. Unlike the fog that slowly rolls out every day about noon on the coast, the fog on his heart lifted instantly. Ok there was a disappointing moment of thinking, assuming, she was married with a few kids. Then she wasn't!

Whoa slow down buddy. He chided himself. *People are drawn to leaders, remember. Don't read into any of Melissa's actions as anything more than friendliness. A smile is just a smile. Fly away hair is just the weather. Zoo animal expressions are just, well, so darn cute!!!*

CHAPTER THIRTY-TWO

Danny, Dad

AND DATING

At the second-hand store, Melissa, the captivating church volunteer, was there. They chatted about the weather. At the grocery store, Melissa was there. Bumping into each other allowed for more dialogue; the weather, what they would cook that night as they checked out each other's basket. Sunday morning greetings, God bless your day. If only they could really talk beyond the surface.

Danny finished wrapping things up on the dock and headed back to the parish. Something was tugging at him, and he wanted to sit quietly with the afternoon sun warming the sanctuary and quiet his soul to listen. But that wasn't how his day went. As he approached the steps to the church, Melissa approached him, concern etched across her face.

"Father Dan, um Danny, I was getting frantic when I couldn't find you. It's Aunt Eleanor. I think it's her meds again. I stopped in for a quick visit and she was on the floor."

"You called 911."

"Yes...yes. They're taking her to the ER. I want to be there but, well you know, my car isn't that reliable." The winding thirty-minute drive to the hospital on the back roads of their coastal town wasn't for the faint of heart or unreliable cars.

"Come on, let me get my keys and we'll both go."

At the ER they found Aunt Eleanor resting, with an IV for fluids to flush her system. The doctor assured them that she was doing well after mixing up her meds and taking the wrong doses. She probably was dehydrated as well. He recommended a follow up with her primary care doctor. A few hours late, Aunt Eleanor was cleared to leave a few hours later.

Melissa and Danny each took one of Aunt Eleanor's arms bracing her as she steadied herself to get into the car for the drive home. It would take 24- 48 hours to get her meds balanced after she had mistakenly taken them incorrectly.

Aunt Eleanor was instantly asleep while the young couple in the front seat were instantly aware that the crisis was averted and they had over thirty minutes until they arrived back in town. Melissa shifted in her seat, looked into the back then smiled at Father Dan, "Thank you. That was very kind of you."

"The next time you want to spend time with me, we could, well maybe, if you'd like, do it over dinner."

"Oh, can a priest do that?"

"Nope. It's totally against my solemn vows."

"That's kind of strict, isn't it?' Melissa glanced over and there was his mischievous smile. "You're teasing me." They both laughed.

"Okay. Dinner it is." Danny was not going to let this opportunity slip by.

Let the dating begin.

Less than an hour later, Aunt Eleanor was home sitting in her favorite chair while Melissa prepared some soup. "Won't you stay and join us?

"That sounds tempting and smells tempting. Sure."

Sitting at the Dock of the Bay resounded louding. Danny saw the caller's name and knew tonight was not going to happen as he had hope.

After he ended the call, he sheepishly said, "It looks like I left a few tasks undone that need my attention. I'd better head out."

As he was saying good bye another phone call interrupted them. He saw it was his mother. He started for the door. Danny mouthed, "I have to take this. Bye."

Melissa nodded as her heart sank at Danny leaving.

"Hi Mom. Dad. What's up."

"It's me Danny, mom. Your dad is pretty worked up. Would you try to calm him down please."

Danny could hear the tension in his mom's voice. "Sure Mom. What's going on?" He got into his car but did not start the engine.

"Oh, you know, all this with Janine."

Danny had a hot or cold relationship with his dad which had finally started to settle in on a consistent warmth since Danny became a pastor and had a church. When he was a kid, his dad never compared him to Janine the star at everything she did. For that Danny was thankful. As the Mayor of Langley, his dad had gotten Danny involved in many events and always seemed proud to introduce him. His dad was highly motivated, like Janine but, unlike Janine, he could get intense.

The downside of his intensity came out when his dad was stressed or upset. That was the thunderbolt temper. That's when Danny and Janine made themselves scarce, if possible. He ranted. He paced like a bull bumping into furniture and tables as décor items met their demise. He got prickly and even critical. Thankfully, he never struck out or was threatening. His ire would run its course in due time. Finally, like throwing a switch, he was good-ole dad again. The venting was over, life was back in harmony, most often helped along by his mom's soothing words. Lately that intercession had become Danny's responsibility. For some reason he could get through to his dad.

Casey's death and Janine running away to Aunt Sally's unnerved his father. Danny suspected that the off-the-grid RV trip was mom's way to create an interim lifestyle that was more serene both in pace and surroundings. A time to heal. It helped but it was not a panacea.

"Hey Dad. How are you doing?"

"Can you believe this. I can't. I just can't. I won't have it. Sure, it's probably good that Janine has come out of her hiding place. Sure. But where is she? Why won't she let us in, let us help? It's the same as it has been all these months. A enormous void. Not knowing."

"Dad how can you, her father, not want to help her, be there for her. I do too. I almost jumped in my car to find her after that first call. But you know Janine..."

"Headstrong!"

"Well, yeh maybe a little. She's also very smart and ridiculously independent."

"How smart is it to cut us all off? Silence. Nothing." His indignation growing.

Tenderly Danny replied, "Come on Dad, you have to admit that she knows her own mind and innately what she needs, emotionally. It's not the way we would do it. I mean entomb at Aunt Sally's. Yet in her own time, with God's help, she has found her way out of that. She texts us every night. When I read her short updates, I truly sense that healing is occurring."

"You do?" Dad His dad said as his melt-down diffused. "I guess you're right. I want so badly to have my daughter back. To do something to make it better for her."

"Well Dad, as you have always taught us, when we can't get it done, we know Jesus is there always, never forsaking us. He's there with Janine and he's touching her soul with his love and grace. Let's keep praying."

"You're right son. And yes, mom and I are praying."

They chatted for a bit longer about non essential happenings. As they said goodnight Danny started his car to head home. The tasks at church could wait until tomorrow. God had choreographed this day, a light unto his path. Danny had willingly followed, the path was laid out before him.

Chapter Thirty-Three

Finally

Danny and Melissa hadn't done it yet. The Date. It was still out there hanging around like Christmas lights in July, waiting for a ladder to be placed against the house. Or for the holidays to start again, whichever came first. Indecision? Life?

Every time Danny had occasion to be near Melissa, he caught himself gazing at her as he practiced in his mind ways to turn words into reality, make the ask, set a date. Yup, indecision. Running scenarios through his mind, he sat across the circle from her on the dunes where the teens had gathered for a bonfire.

"Um Father Dan, you, okay?" Asked Tricia, one of the teens sitting near him. "You have a funny look on your face."

"Sure. Yes. Fine. My thoughts were a million miles away."

"More like across the way. Who are you checkin' out?"

"Checkin' out. No, no. Except to keep my eye on Grant or he'll try to sneak off again." The fifteen-year-old was sitting next to Melissa. *"Good save Danny"* he said to himself.

"You got that right. This time Lisa will follow. They're together now."

"Together. Really. I never saw that coming."

"No one ever sees love coming Father Dan. It just whams you in the heart."

Danny looked at Tricia. Where did this 13-year-old, bookish, tomboy gain such astute insight on matters of the heart. She sure got it right though. Danny met Melissa and WHAM!!

Without him knowing, Melissa moved right behind him. "Hey Father…. Tricia. Hate to break up your conversation but it's time for s'mores and I can't find the main ingredient, marshmallows. The kids made sticks, we have about 10 boxes of graham crackers and way too much chocolate. But no marshmallows."

Danny shook his head. "Oh dang, did I leave them in my truck? Probably. Let me go back up to the parking lot and check."

"Here, let me go with you." Melissa offered.

Away they went, leaving the chatter and laughter of teens behind them. Well, with a few older teens around to prevent any misadventures. "Brad, Rochelle keep an eye on thigs until we get back." Dan called out.

Sure enough, the marshmallows were right where Danny had left them, "So they wouldn't get squashed." He held them up triumphantly.

"It worked." Melissa pronounced, "They are all plump and healthy. What do ya think, will there be any chocolate left by the time we get back?"

"There'd better be! That's the best part."

"No. No. No. The gooey almost burnt marshmallow, that's the best part."

"Dripping, melting chocolate beats gooey every time."

They picked up their pace both with mouths watering thinking about their favorite part of a s'more.

They headed back in a marching motion to move as fast as possible with thick sand grabbing at their ankles. Alone in the semi-dark, close enough to hear Melissa's breathing, Danny reached toward her hand but stopped. First things first. It struck Danny that this would be a good time to ask

Melissa out to dinner, away from a crowd of people. No more chit-chat. The time was now.

"Um." He cleared his throat. "I wanted to ask you if...."

"I know. You want me to help start a Sunday school class for the five-year-old kids. Right?"

"Huh? No. I want to marry you and have lots of children."

The ocean crashed. An owl hooted. In the distance, faint laughter rose up from the group of teens. Melissa stopped dead in her tracks and turned toward Danny looking him straight in the eye.

"Yikes. I really said that. Oh, Mellissa I am sooo sorry. I mean...I didn't mean...well it's just that..."

"Danny, if you want me to have your children don't you think we ought to start by at least going on a date or something like that. You know, be old fashion??"

"Yes. Old fashion. Absolutely. Great idea."

"But then again, why bother, we both know how this will end."

"With our children?"

"Nope. We'll never get that far. If you like dripping chocolate over gooey marshmallow, any relationship is doomed before it starts."

Danny dropped the shopping bag filled with marshmallows and put both hands over his heart, "I'll swear off chocolate if you'll have dinner with me tomorrow night."

"Sure. Deal." She looked at Danny's stunned expression, "Oh, did I answer too fast?"

Danny gave her a quick kiss on the cheek, grabbed the sack as they headed toward the teens to let them eat even more sugar than they had so far. It was a great night. High on sugar and love.

WHAM.

CHAPTER THIRTY-FOUR

Mother

AND DAUGHTER

After spending the morning with Millie and George, I was in no rush to find my next destination. My drive was more leisurely than I had planned when I first awoke that morning. I caught myself drifting into thoughts; remembering the morning and how it felt to talk about my tragedy.

"I learned something today, Peaches." I said out loud because I just had to speak, "First that this is not "my" tragedy alone. Many people lost Casey."

I looked at my furry passenger, who was staring back intently, *"Me too, I miss that little ear-puller."*

"Even worse is that I shut everyone out. We needed each other and I was oblivious to anyone else's pain. Mine was so all-consuming."

As I drove, snapshots of those first few days came into focus. I saw the grief and sorrow that was undeniably etched in the faces of those I loved; Ken, my parents, his parents, my baby brother trying so hard to be there for me even while their own eyes shattered like glass, mirroring their broken hearts. Hollow. Hopeless. Empty. Pain-filled. Lost. Fearful. All those eyes.

All that sadness. It was too much sorrow to absorb. It's no wonder I shut down,

Even a few months later; Aunt Sally tried to hide her distress when I, her disheveled niece, showed up at her. "Janine, what are you..." She caught herself mid-sentence. She knew what had driven me to her door. "Come in."

"Can I stay here Aunt Sally?" I had said, more an explanation than a request, as I wandered down the hall to the guest room, flopped on the bed and immediately fell asleep. Peaches jumped up on the bed next to me. Being awake, pretending to be alive depleted all my energy. There was nothing left within me; sleep was my hiding place. Have you ever been there?

"As long as you need dear, as long as you need." Aunt Sally said to me, a I laid sound-asleep. She slipped off my runners, placed a blanket over me, a bowl of water on the floor and stepped out, quietly closing the door.

Now as I drove my camper van, I was starting to remember. To my relief I did not feel the need to shut out the memories. I spoke out each one's name with a quick thought held up to God for the heartache they had felt, are probably still feeling and how I might have had added to their sorrow.

"The other thing I learned today, Peaches," I looked again to my right and saw that Peaches was still listening, which warmed my heart, "...is that I am not the only one that has faced tragedy in life. Millie and George have been through so much yet, there they are cherishing every minute, embracing every new day like a precious gift. They aren't hiding but instead they are loving others. Including me."

Peaches added, *"And me."*

I positioned my Bluetooth on my ear and hit my speed dial.

"Hello."

"Mom, it's me."

"Yes, I see that."

"Ah, you're getting used to checking your caller ID."

"I am a millennial woman now, Janine." My mother said with pride. "How are you. Where are you?'

"Is dad there too?"

"He went into town to get a few supplies."

"Mom how did you feel when Ken called you and Dad?"

When her mom heard that question, for the first time since Casey's death, her heart welled-up with hope. Had her daughter made it through that dark shadow they had all been forced to walk? She had prayed that one day her only daughter could speak of their shared tragedy. Was this the day?

"Shocked, with a gripping searing pain that ripped through my heart. Like every organ inside of me turned into hot coals. I remember just crying out. Holding my hands over my mouth as I screamed." My mother said without holding back. "Thankfully your father was close by. When he heard me, he quickly led me to the couch as he took the phone from me."

After a moment of hesitation, she continued, "I just sat there waiting for your dad to tell me I had misunderstood. That it was an accident. That Casey would be fine."

"Me too. I kept saying, no...no...no. I wanted someone to tell me it was all a mistake."

"I kept thinking what I could bring to the hospital to wait with you and Ken."

Seeing a side street, I made a quick turn then pulled off the road knowing I was going to cry again. We both cried. Mother and daughter. We shared and let out all that had been left unsaid for far too long.

As the conversation started to wind down, my mom knew she could finally say it. She told me, "Baby, losing Casey was the most horrible thing I thought I would ever have to face. But losing you. That was too much to bear."

"Oh Mom...I am so sorry. I was lost. No, I wasn't even alive. I died with my little girl, my sweet, sweet Casey."

"Yes, that is what happened isn't it? My two treasures, both, lost."

I did more than stopped living. A few months after the memorial I had gotten on a plane with not much more than a duffle stuffed with whatever was around my unkempt bedroom, mostly unwashed clothes. Peaches rode in a tote slung over my shoulder. I walked out the door, turned around and went back in to jot a cryptic note to Ken. "I left. There's nothing inside of me."

At Aunt Sally's I rarely ventured out. I didn't eat much. I slept in between crying jags for months. I wanted to be alone during that time, but my parents had arrived at my aunt's. Mom held me, soothed me, tried to comfort her only daughter. I kept pushing her away. My parents had brought along my bike, some of my belongings and favorite mementos as a reminder that I had a life.

"I need space Mom. Give me some space."

"I love you, Janine. Let me help you through this."

In answer, I rolled away from where my mother stood and pulled the covers completely over myself, mumbling inaudibly.

I heard Aunt Sally as she took her sister Pam's hand gently drawing her out of my room. "She'll come through this Pam, she's safe here. She has to find her own way, grieve in her own way. It seems to be that she doesn't want either of us hovering. At least not right now."

"Oh Sally, Janine's my baby. I feel so helpless."

From that place of utter helplessness, the two sisters would do the only thing they could, hold each other and pray as tears cascaded down their faces. I faintly heard them as they poured out their hearts in fragile words of crushed hopes and lost dreams; of pleadings and yearnings; sometimes even anger at the unfairness of it all. Sometimes my dad's voice joined them.

Once I heard my mom slide down the wall to sit on the floor, in the hallway, by the door that held me, her broken daughter captive. Sit and wait. In vain. Always in vain.

"I knew you were sitting in the hall by the door. I couldn't move, respond. I was in an emotional coma."

"I was trying to push my prayers through the barrier that separated me from you, my hurting child."

Although Pam wanted it, she thought this day would never come, a day when Janine would come out from her solitary world to engage in life once again. Even when she had first headed off in that camper van, Pam thought it was just another diversion from facing life.

When her phone rang and the caller ID came up with Janine's name, Pam had braced herself for another fruitless call full of short answers with no substance. Yet she had found that not only was she conversing with her daughter she was hearing a different tone in Janine's voice. The child she had thought was lost to her forever was speaking in a voice that quivered with life.

They candidly shared their slow labored trek through their stony wall of sorrow. It was not with voices walking into that cavernous valley. Instead, it was with voices that were walking out of that dark lonely place, like they were walking up out of a cold, damp, windowless prison.

"You sound good Janine. Even as we shared all we have both been carrying." Pam said as their conversation was drawing to an end.

"Oh Mom, I …I…. this is just what I needed. I think I am starting to come alive again."

"Yes baby, I think you are. Janine, hearing your voice is like music. The best worship music ever."

"I love you, Mom."

"I love you, my dear child."

"Ah mom. I'll call you again later when Dad's home."

"Oh Jani, that would be great. Your Dad would love to hear from you."

As the call ended, each woman remained where they were, still, wrapped tenderly in words of understanding and reconciliation. Love found a way.

"Jesus loves me, no no no..."
Janine melted at the sound of Casey's whimsical
four-year-old voice singing as they drove home from church.
She kept driving past the turn toward their home
just to hear the sound of Casey's voice,
like a tinkling harp, filling her ears.
Janine began to sing along,
"Jesus loves me this I know...."
Mommy. Mommy. Stop. You have the wrong words.
Listen to me. You can do it.
"Jesus loves me no, no no..."
So, they sang Casey's version.
There was not a more lovely duet in all the land.

CHAPTER THIRTY-SIX

Benchmark

It was still May when Ken exclaimed, "I got it!" before Danny could finish saying hello. "A bench. I'm going to make a bench. It will be perfect." Ken sounded both excited and edgy.

"Yo bro, ok a bench. Why all the excitement?"

"You were right..." Ken began to explain but Danny quipped, "Well of course."

Ken kept talking, "...awhile ago, do you remember what you said to me?"

"Something timely and very wise?"

"Yes!" Ken paused, thankful that he had reached out to Danny when the thought of Casey's birthday was weighing heavily on him. It would be her first birthday since the accident. Their talk had not only helped by allowing Ken to vent, but he had been inspired by Danny's words of advice.

Danny was completely baffled, wracking his brain to remember what he had said but he was drawing a blank. He finally had to admit it, "Uh, Ken, what are you talking about?"

"You said to do something to remember Casey, to start a tradition or something that would make her birthday a positive experience each year."

Slowly the comment started to come back to Danny. It had just been a quick thought at a point to redirect Ken after vented. It was not this momentous piece of wisdom. Well, ok maybe.

"A bench?" he said to hear more of Ken's idea.

"I am going to make a bench to put at a local park, even Dungeness Spit if they let me, in honor of Casey. Kind of "In Memory of." I'm thinking of teak. It'll withstand the weather."

"Man, that's perfect. That's terrific. What a fantastic idea!"

"Well, it was your doing. Thanks bro."

"Hey, every now and then I astound even myself! But really Ken, let me know when you have it done. Better yet send me pictures as you are creating this. Knowing you it will be a masterpiece."

"Sure thing. I'm thinking of teak combined with treated branches up the side or the back. I'll know better which way to go when I have the wood. Maybe some design or something on the back, the part that you rest against. I've been sketching all morning."

"Ya know I've got a bucket of sand dollars that Casey made with the vacation Bible school kids when she stayed with me for that week. How 'bout I send you a few of those, if you can use them."

"Send them for sure. Oh, and how 'bout a scripture verse. You're good at that Danny?"

"I could do that or help you choose. Nah, you do it. Your heart will guide you." Danny wanted it to be Ken's expression to the memory of Casey, his daughter. A verse that spoke to Ken would be better than any he could offer.

"Maybe I can add other things that were special to Casey." Ken was thinking out loud while he scribbled on his design pad. He got so intent on what he was writing he forgot he was even on the phone.

Danny heard Ken talking to himself as Ken's pencil moved across the paper, "Earth to Ken. Gotta go man, send me pictures."

"Oh yeh, will do. Danny, thanks. Really thanks. You're the best." He said as he hung up.

Chapter Thirty-Seven

Soup's On

At their home in Sequim on the Olympic Peninsula, Sofia hung up the phone just as Felix was lumbering in through the back door wiping his brow.

"Planters and annuals are done." He said with little pride at the yard work he had been doing for the past several hours. "I'm getting too old for this; it just isn't fun anymore."

Sofia cut him off, "Before you start trying to sell me on a gardener, let me tell you about the call I just got."

That peaked Felix's interest, but food was first on his mind as he opened the fridge and starred at its contents, "I'm gonna get something to eat while you tell all."

"No, no. This is too important. Here, let me warm up the leftover enchiladas from last night." She said edging past him, nudging him out of my way with her hip.

Felix readily stepped back, always willing to let Sofia do her magic in the kitchen. As Sofia started gathering plastic containers of the leftovers that she had put in the fridge the night before, Felix got out a glass and began to fill it with water. "Are you going to eat?"

"I had a late breakfast. Theresa stopped over. So, I'm good."

"Theresa huh. What's the important news? Did she find a husband on E-Harmony yet?" Theresa, a young widow, who worked with Sofia, was ready to marry again. She knew everyone in Sequim, so she broadened her reach by going online via E-Harmony in the hopes of finding true love, someone to marry and share the rest of their lives together.

Sofia placed the leftovers on a plate and put them in the microwave, setting it for two minutes. "Not yet," she answered, "but there are a few potential MR's." She giggled as she thought about her girl-time with Theresa. "The important news though, is the phone call I just got from Ken."

"Ken? Langley Ken?" Felix said a bit astonished. It had been quite a while since they had last spoken to Ken. Calls usually happened when they initiated it. Ken was always pleasant, polite, even kind but he usually seemed to be holding back. Not at all unexpected.

The microwave beeped at them. Sofia got out the food, while Felix grabbed a fork and they both sat down at the kitchen table.

"Gracias, mi amor. Now tell all. Mmmm, this smells great." Felix said as he sent his fork in for a landing.

Felix and Sofia were retired, well, semi-retired, after years working at churches across the western hemisphere. Because they were bilingual, they had even been missionaries for three years in Guatemala. Felix was a pastor, while Sofia was a nurse which was a perfect fit for the mission field in Guatemala where they had gone to share the gospel while establishing a walk-in clinic.

Since then and all through Felix's time as a pastor, state-side, they had gone on yearly mission trips to minister to the medical and spiritual needs of people in South America. They considered themselves semi-retired because Sofia and Felix spent the summer camping around western Washington while serving as the chaplain in campgrounds, leading inter-denominational services on Sundays. They stayed anywhere from a month to the entire summer season.

They had two grown sons: one a pastor and the other following in Sofia's footsteps as a nurse. Taking it further, he was studying to become a nurse-practitioner so he could be even more involved in the health of people.

Felix had been a street kid from the New York City barrio who found refuge and acceptance in a gang. Sofia had grown up in the same neighborhood, they had even gone to the same school, but their lives were worlds apart. Then one day their two worlds collided when a punk was talking rudely and throwing trash at this slight, pretty girl minding her own business as she walked down the street. It was Sofia. Felix came to her defense and stood his ground against the punk, who turned out to be the brother of a rival gang member.

First off, the thug was outside his territory; second off he was messin' with an innocent. In one swift move Felix put him on the ground. With the harasser at Felix's feet, he looked at the girl before him and with bravado announced that she was free to pass. Ah the gallantry, he thought.

Sofia just pushed past and petulantly exclaimed, "Oh grow up why don't you!"

A minor gang skirmish ensued, the standard tit-for-tat, posturing, mouthing off but it didn't go very far, just far enough for Felix to see himself as Sofia had seen him. He found he agreed with her; it was time to grow up.

His first step was to seek out Reverent Nick, another former street kid turned good. It was under the good Rev's tutelage that Felix decided he too wanted to learn how to do good in the world. He felt that he had taken so much from the streets of New York that now he wanted to give something back.

Rev Nick had heard many gang members talk a good talk, but few followed through with actions. His first test was the soup kitchen where he put the newly converted to work. Well, more like free labor, peeling hundreds of potatoes all morning to add substance to the soup. If anyone came back the next week he gave them carrot duty. Peeling and slicing hundreds of carrots. It always gave him a good laugh to see these big burly tough guys trying to hold onto a carrot, peal it, then slice it, at an angle.

The soup kitchen weeded out more than it graduated. That was not the case with Felix. He never gave up on his desire to be a better person. There was an additional incentive for Felix sticking with it and that was getting to the point when he would be placed at the front tables just outside of the kitchen to serve.

Yes, up front, the chores were easier, and you got to interact with the people you were there for a meal. But, from the very first day at the soup kitchen Felix had his own motivation. While hauling a 50-pound sack of potatoes in, from Rev Nick's truck, he had seen his damsel in distress. Or rather, that uppity mouthy girl he had tried to rescue the month before. Her voiced still echoed in his mind, "Oh grow up why don't you!"

That was exactly what he was doing. At first, he thought he could impress her with his culinary skills, until he discovered he didn't have any such skills. Peeling vegetables did not seem remarkable. Then he thought his strength could be what she would see. After carrying hundreds of pounds of potatoes in, peeling them along with a few swipes of his fingers, and cutting them into quarters, the only thing he could muster up was sweat. He probably stank too. It was probably better to stay in the back where he wouldn't offend anyone.

Felix concluded he had to work his way to the top, or to the front. By night he was inspired by Rev Nick and what he was learning at the young men's Bible study. By day, well once a week, he was inspired by his goal to get promoted to the front of the soup kitchen. It took three months. By then his attitude had changed, his heart had softened, and a newfound faith had begun to reach into his soul.

During that time, he had also learned the girl's name, Sofia. She was a freshman in college studying to become a nurse. He no longer wanted to redeem himself, to show how tough he was or to have Sofia grovel at his feet and feel foolish for having said what she had said. No, he was now determined to know who she was, what drew her to the soup kitchen and what was in her soul. The essence of all she embodied.

When he thought of a question that he could ask her to start a conversation like, "What is your favorite Bible verse..." It felt too much like the old pick-up line. *Hey baby, what's your Zodiac sign."*

For the first time, he had to admit, that he felt intimidated by a woman, by Sofia. A thought he had never had before. He always knew he could take whatever woman he wanted; it was his right as the gang mentality had taught him. Heck, he didn't even have to use a come-on line to impose himself on a woman.

After seeing himself as Sofia had seen him, he knew he had to give up all that he was. He had to walk away from the street life that he thought would make him someone. By the grace of God and with the help of Rev Nick he could start life anew, this time with faith in Christ as his foundation. Funny, he didn't hesitate in considering a new life, of giving up all he had known for many years. This time hope propelled him, it would sustain him and refine him.

He used to snicker at people who needed religion. Oh, they were so weak. Funny what you do when you are empty inside and trying to pretend you had it all together. Bravado and aggressiveness covers a lot of what he didn't have. After placing his trust in Christ, he felt his personhood grow as he stood on that solid rock of faith; well, at any rate he was learning how to stand on that rock and not fall off, too much anyway. The view from there was completely different and he was feeling that difference deep inside himself.

During his three-month stint in the kitchen Felix had gotten very adept at carrots and potatoes, along with onions, celery, zucchini, and whatever other fresh vegetables had been donated. Thanksgiving week was upon them and the kitchen was bustling to prepare extra food and some special treats for their guests. The holidays drew many more volunteers and as newbies they were assigned to prep work in the kitchen.

This led to Rev Nick's directive, "Hey, Felix, how 'bout you go up front and help out the servers?"

"Done!" Felix replied with his dirty apron off before the word left his mouth. Then he froze. His mouth went dry. The front. Sofia. Three months of stolen glances and wrestling through his feelings; coming to grips with his new faith while still trying to slow his heart rate down when he saw her. Did she know he was there? Did she even remember who he was?

"Hey Felix, get on a clean apron and move it. It'll be filling up out there fast."

"On my way boss." He said with more confidence than he felt. Confidence? Felix pushed through the swinging door and walked right up toward where Sofia was trying to serve a growing crowd of people.

He tied the apron strings behind his back asking, "How can I help?"

They were part of three serving stations, each getting busier by the minute.

"Here, you serve the turkey, corn, and potatoes. Pass it to me and I'll add gravy, bread and salad." she responded without even looking up from what she was doing.

Bossy broad, um woman, Felix thought as he began filling plates and passing them along to her. As he worked with and watched Sofia, he knew all his images of what she would be like were wrong. The reason for his somewhat distorted view of women, he realized, was because he continued to find the barnacles of his former life clinging to him.

He shook his head as if to free himself from the wrong thoughts in his mind and began to appraise Sofia in real time. Still petite, she hadn't grown a speck, with soft olive skin and gray-brown eyes that drew you to look her straight in the face. Sofia exuded a feisty confidence. Felix saw this trait in action the faster she worked.

Her sing-song voice took on more precision as she thought quickly and directed those around her, making no apologies for the work that had to get done fast and efficiently. Just as quickly she could turn toward a person waiting in line and speak in soothing, caring tones, tenderness lighting her face to make the most wretched person feel welcome.

"He saved a wretch like me." Felix recalled the refrain from the song Amazing Grace. Thank you, Father.

Felix had a hint of that in-charge side of Sofia, which did not deter him one bit. He had some confidence as well. Even after having to change his image of Sofia, defining who she truly was rather than the fantasy he had built up over the last few months, he was still drawn to her. No, it was more than that. He felt compelled to win her over, to one day share his life fully with her.

Sofia on the other hand had her own plans which did not include a man, especially the big lump of showmanship working next to her. It was fine when he was back in the kitchen. He'd even done a much better job than she had ever expected. Add to that, Rev Nick could not say enough good about him.

But Sofia always pulled back from showy people, guys even more so. All talk and not much else. She caught the contradiction in her thoughts. This guy was more than talk. He had stuck around when most never made it through Rev Nick's boot camp. He took action each time she made everyone pick up the pace.

Friendly. He was so friendly to the people who came into the soup kitchen, like they were family. He was good looking with his dark skin, dark eyes and even darker, jet-black hair. But he was huge, look at those hands she thought. His muscular arms were larger than her leg.

After her last of several heartbreaks, she finally came to see what her friends had seen all along; she had horrible taste in men. Nursing school, church, hanging with friends [girls only, thank you] and volunteering, was where she was putting her energies. Time with friends was not spent at parties or wherever men would be. If a man was there, she was not. How else could she avoid making yet another wrong choice? She liked men but it became all too obvious that she liked all the wrong men. Done. Over. The end.

Sofia was living in her no-man zone and enjoying life. She liked being without all the tension of a relationship and trying to figure out who she was when someone else was so prominent in her life. Expectations. Growing together without losing herself; she always lost herself. Bad choices.

This past year of being unattached allowed her to be exactly who she wanted to be or didn't want to be on any given day. She was happily content and was not crushed by the loneliness she feared would dominate her days.

It took Felix four weeks, working side-by-side with Sofia during the holidays, to get her to joke and laugh with him. She could be so open and caring with the people. She handed plates of food to people or sat down to chat moving from table to table. Yet, she would put up a wall whenever the work pace slowed, and Felix tried to engage her in conversation. Finally, she laughed. Almost.

"I saw that smile. You were gonna laugh." He said letting out a long laugh himself. A full-sized man's laugh reverberated across the room.

Rev Nick and the others were laughing too. Sofia joined in, letting down her guard. After all, it was Christmas and she was in a light-hearted, holiday frame of mind. Felix grinned; he had finally broken through her guarded exterior. Her laugh was like a thousand crystal wind chimes, awakened by a gentle breeze.

All these years later she still would proclaim, "Felix, you big goof, you could always make me laugh."

"Sofia, you were born to laugh. Your laughter is music to my heart."

After all these years of marriage, Felix sat at the table eating lunch, but remembering to make eye contact [oh how he could still get lost in Sofia's eyes] as she began to tell him about her conversation with Ken.

"First off, Ken sounded good, really good." Sofia started. "I think some real healing has happened since the last time we spoke to him. Casey's birthday is coming and Ken's birthday. He was getting himself all wound up and upset about it. Then he talked to Danny..."

"Danny, that's Janine's brother?" Felix asked.

"Yes, Janine's brother. He's the priest that lives on the Oregon coast. I guess Danny made a comment that Ken might want to do something in memory of Casey. You know, kind of soften the tragedy, don't let what happen always take away the good times that were there."

"Pretty sound advice, I'd say."

"Well, we have also had to do that. We fought to do that."

"We prayed hard, cried hard and came broken and shattered leaning on God to get us there."

"Yes, we did." Sofia paused as they both remember how they had finally felt God's answer to their personal side-trip through hell.

Chapter Thirty-Eight

In Just

Seconds

On that tragic day that Casey had died, Felix and Sofia had been headed to the Dungeness Spit campground to set up and stay for a three-months with Felix commissioned to lead Sunday worship. Sofia was going to volunteer in the town of Sequim at a free clinic for the duration.

It had been a while since Sofia had done any nursing, mostly because they had been traveling around since Felix became a campground chaplain. She had a habit of going online to read the newspaper of whatever town or city they would be serving in next to search for volunteer nursing opportunities. While reading the Sequim Gazette paper she came across an article about the clinic there and its need for temporary volunteers during their peak summer season with hundreds of migrant workers in town. Even though Felix and Sofia would only be in the area for three months she decided to call and offer her services. Sofia and the clinic director hit it off and the fact that Sofia was bilingual sealed the deal. She had herself a job. Volunteering, using her skills to help others. Sofia never made it to her scheduled first day.

Their day of travel to Dungeness Spit had been one of those days that started out perfectly then promptly spiraled downward, one incident after another. When they finally reached Sequim, they got lost trying to find the campground. They asked for directions after maneuvering their truck and fifth-wheel around several one-way streets, and started toward the state park, only to get lost again.

When they finally found the campground and checked in, they both exhaled a deep sigh of relief. Bone tired and road weary, Sofia thought about the pre-made dinner that awaited them in the refrigerator. No need to cook. They just had to park the trailer and while Felix did the outside set up, she would heat up the salsa-verde chicken casserole. In fact, she would suggest to Felix that they could eat and catch their breath before doing all the hook-ups. She could see he was worn out as well.

Instead, tragedy struck.

Instead, they caused a tragedy.

Before the trailer was parked. Before the dinner was served. Before any clinic work was done. A little girl named Casey had lost her life.

How do you crawl out from under the wreckage of such loss? Casey couldn't. Could they? How do you find any solace when a child has died by your own doing?

For Felix and Sofia, it took a long time. There was no time. Just waking. Not wanting to be awake; plodding through the day, with no energy, just doing something, pretending to be doing something. Then grateful that another day was over, and sleep, aided by a pill, could close in to stop the vivid memories. That is, if they could sleep. Many nights they could not and laid in each other's arms crying softly, praying.

The memories were a knotted clump of rope, always with the same ending; the fresh smell of the ocean air and the soothing sound of the early evening tide until they were suddenly overtaken by the thud of impact, the screams, the cries, and the sight of a precious child as life left her little body.

CHAPTER THIRTY-NINE

A Small

MEASURE OF COMFORT

Somewhere within the bitter cold grief that enshrouded Sofia and Felix, God had begun to speak to them. At first it was a mere word, *Ricco*, whose tender warmth thawed the tip of the iceberg that stabbed at their hearts. *Ricco.*

Though he couldn't yet face the loss of Casey, Felix could talk about his brother, even Ricco's death. As they sat one night, in the living room with a warm fire glowing they remembered.

Years ago, Felix and Sofia had just come back from their last and final mission trip to Guatemala. They had accepted an offer to serve in Colorado Springs as an interim pastor. What made that offer easy to accept was the fact that Felix's youngest brother, Ricco, lived just half an hour south of Denver. Ricco was nine years younger, which when they were growing up separated their worlds.

With those many years already between them, it was almost a given that Felix and Ricco had lost contact as they each entered adulthood. This opportunity, the move to Denver, had Felix looking forward to establishing a kinship with his brother.

The reunion surpassed each brother's expectations. Ricco was single, had never married and as a result had all the toys a man could want. He had excelled in his choice of a military career and now ran his own security business, even having his own plane.

With a build similar to Felix as a young man, Ricco had gone further than Felix by transforming his hulking youthful body into a muscular, weight-lifting fit powerhouse. With military discipline he had maintained that strength, whereas Felix's older physique had softened. Let's face it, Felix didn't work as hard to keep himself toned.

When they were reunited, any stranger on the street could tell they were family with their distinctive faces, espresso eyes, thick wavy charcoal colored hair and grins that could serve as lighthouses.

"Hey, my man, you gave up your stash?" Ricco joked as he ran a finger over his own neatly trimmed mustache.

"My lady-killer, yup, don't need it. I've got the best lady there is." Felix said putting his arm around Sofia's waist and pulling her closer.

"So, you do. Now I know why I never married. You got the best and I never settle."

They began to make up for lost time; Ricco proudly showing off all of Colorado and sharing the thrill of all his toys. They went boating, fishing, snowmobiling, and even flying in Ricco's Bombardier jet.

In return, Felix and Sofia gave Ricco the comforts of home and family life as Ricco embraced uncle-ship and spent time with his two nephews. Ricco was even somewhat enthusiastic about joining the family at church and listening to his big brother preach.

Three years later, Ricco was diagnosed with lung cancer, though he had never smoked one cigarette since his early teens. It was because of his healthy habits that his doctor had never suspected lung cancer when Ricco started complaining about being out of breath after working out at the gym. By the time the problem became evident the cancer was too far along to do anything but take a desperate stab at chemo. Ricco chose to enjoy the days he had left rather than spend what time he had in and out of the hospital. "Another round of chemo isn't for me. I can accept death." He often said when asked.

It all happened quickly; the months fell away like hail, hard and chilling. Felix and Sofia helped Ricco move into their spare room. Little did Ricco know that Felix, in his study just down the hall, prayed for his little brother continuously.

"Lord Jesus, you have been so faithful to me. You have been with me at every turn. Ricco has not had that, did not think he wanted a relationship with you, his creator. I can sense the spiritual yearning in Ricco. I pray, my Jesus, that he will be open to who you are. To your peace, grace, forgiveness, mercy and the joy you can pour into a seeking soul. You put within each of us a yearning to know our Creator, to know you. I pray that Ricco will know you."

During the last week of his life Ricco, with a voice barely above a whisper, asked, "Tell me about Jesus. I can see how he has changed your life, Felix. Come on bro, what's the secret, tell me."

Felix did just that. He started right from the beginning recounting his time with Rev Nick and the soup kitchen. He shared from his heart the hope and healing that had come into his life, through faith in Christ, during those months. Felix in his straightforward manner recalled the time when he felt abandoned by God after Sofia's second miscarriage and how they had given up hope of ever having children. How Jesus has reassured him that they would have children, no matter what the doctors were telling them.

Ricco smiled weakly whispering, "And I would have two nephews." Felix was thankful that their two boys had really gotten to know their uncle during these last few years.

When Felix was done sharing about the saving grace of Christ he felt he had said too much. He saw that Ricco's breathing was shallow, his eyes were closed. He got up quietly to leave. Ricco, barely audible said, "Don't go."

Felix sat back down and took Ricco's extended hand.

"I have so much." Ricco said, "all... all just toys. I want what really counts. Peace. Je.... Jesus."

Felix gently placed his other hand over Ricco's and asked, "Do you want to pray."

"Help me." Ricco murmured.

With tears caught in his throat Felix prayed, hearing Ricco murmur as he acknowledged Jesus, the son of God, as his savior. Ricco's face reflected the peace that had entered his soul. Felix quietly spoke at his brother's side throughout the night, holding Ricco's bony hand as he reminisced out loud. He even shared some of his life before Ricco was even born. By the break of new day, Ricco took his last breath.

At the memorial service for Ricco, the chapel was overflowing. Just a Felix shared the hope of Christ with Ricco, after telling a few light hearted stories about his little brother, he shared about how God gave his only begotten son that anyone who believed in him could have everlasting life. Eternity. Where they would even get to see Ricco again. Many of Ricco's friends thanked Felix afterwards as they shared a Ricco story then hugged Felix, Sofia and the boys.

In the present, as they sat together at home in Sequin, being warmed by the fire, they marveled at all God had done. It was Sofia who brought clarity to the loss she, Felix and their sons had felt back then.

She leaned over and said, "Remember when you accepted this position in Colorado? We thought it was about a struggling church that needed strong leadership. You felt the church had no identity and that you could show them who they were with Christ at the center. We thought a side benefit would be getting to see Ricco."

She paused as Felix nodded, remembering. He responded. "That church was so filled with resentfulness. With the we-don't-want-change mentality and a core of mean-spirited people, the failing church was their own doing. Even then I doubted that I could have made a difference. Though we sure tried for several years. I truly didn't understand why God sent us to that church."

In a hushed tone, Sofia went on, "I think we got that a bit backwards. I think God used the church as a lure. The real reason you, we, were brought there was because God knew that Ricco would need us. And he would want to know Jesus."

Felix turned to look at Sofia's wise face, the truth of those past few years striking him powerfully within his soul. He gently squeezed her hand, "And we needed Ricco."

"Yes. Yes, we did." Sofia said, "The verse in Romans says it best. All things work together for good for those who love the Lord."

Of course he knew this, in his scripture-educated mind. But his heart had to be open to receive that truth. God knew that all things, good and bad, joyful or even suffering could work for good. It was knowing, with absolute certainty, that God did indeed have a reason, multiple reasons, for the way He moved in their lives. Even through the grieving, they were filled with the peace of Jesus that surpassed their understanding.

Leaning into God had gotten them through the loss of Ricco; not just through it, but they began to have a renewed desire to reach out to more people, to minister to the broken, hurting and even the dying. Both Felix and Sofia got involved with the local Hospice chapter and were blessed to help many prepare for their final journey in life. With deep joy they prayed with those who asked for prayer knowing they were about to meet their Heavenly Father face to face. On earth they saw through a mirror dimly. Soon they would see clearly. For those who were not comfortable with prayer, they sat with them and cared for them. They found that by being there and listening, the dying let them know what they needed to vanquish their fears or concerns. Felix and Sofia responded with what a person needed, reading poetry, bringing in a favorite painting, giving one person a sip of wine; whatever brought them comfort.

Ricco's death was a good twenty years ago. Felix and Sofia had stayed in Colorado albeit at a much more hospitable church. In fact, the three years of hostility in that first church prepared Felix to be better pastor in the next church where is ministered for seventeen years.

Felix semi-retired and they began their new life as gypsies. Traveling and staying at campgrounds where Felix would be the chaplain for the season and Sofia would help out at a local clinic, if there was an opening. These pursuits had filled their hearts with purpose as they met many delightful people with every assignment.

Until the dreadful trip to Dungeness Spit. The Spit brought about another death, another life lost, a child's life. An accident, everyone would agree, but it was at Felix's hands that an innocent life was lost. The grief was immeasurable.

As Felix, then Sofia began to emerge from that pit of despair, they held onto to each other. As they reached out for God's strong hand of healing, they remembered the loss of Ricco. In doing so, they remembered that God was always faithful. What was true back then was true for their current feelings of despair. They could stay stuck in this hollow cold crevasse of grief or they could ask God to lift them out and use them.

Reflecting on their time in Colorado, they both came to understand that there was more to this heart crushing accident and Casey's death. Beyond all they felt right now, God could use this if they would let him.

They started pray for God to show them what good could come from such tragedy.

CHAPTER FORTY

We Can Help

After the accident, Felix and Sofia decided to stay in Sequim. There was a time of healing. But what also helped was when the pastor at the church they had been attending asked Felix to cover for him one Sunday. From then on Felix covered for many of the local pastors when they were ill, on retreat or taking time off. Felix doing what he loved was a balm to his soul.

Just as Felix needed to minster, Sofia's desire to help others drew her back to that clinic. She re-connected with the director and became the part time RN, filling a position recently vacated.

Sitting in the kitchen, their conversation about Ken's call continued. After a few bites of the reheated leftovers, Felix looked up at Sofia, prompting her to finish telling him about the call from Ken. "You say, even with Casey's birthday coming, Ken was sounding good?"

"Yes. Oh, Felix, it was something to hear him. We were just chatting like normal people. With buoyancy in his voice, Ken told me in some detail about a way honor of Casey."

They had tried to make contact with Ken and Janine several months after the tragedy, only to find out that Janine had left Ken. When a few other calls went unanswered, they decided to let it go. They maintained a vigil of prayers for the young couple. Could this be their answer?

Felix's curiosity was peaked, "What's this about a memorial to honor Casey?"

"Well, you know Ken is part of his dad's wood working shop. He is going to make a bench in honor of Casey. He wants to have it placed in a park. At first, he was thinking of a park in Langley where he lives. Then he mentioned Dungeness Spit, the campground where it all happened"

"We can help him with that. I know Curtis over at parks and rec. I am sure he would know who to contact to get permission to put a bench there."

"Yes, dear. That's exactly what I was thinking. Mostly though, just hearing Ken's voice with a touch of joy and lightness in it. All the planning is great, but hearing his voice was so encouraging."

"We both know there will be good days and bad days for Ken. Janine too. A memorial bench for Casey is part of the path toward recovery for Ken. Ah, yes. Very encouraging."

Felix's mind was going in several directions. He felt a strong urge to be more involved with this project, yet he didn't want to interfere in Ken's life. In the end Felix called Ken, and they too had a good talk. Felix felt comfortable asking if he and Sofia could have a sandblasted plaque made for the bench. Ken was touched by his offer and the two men began throwing out ideas as to the wording on the plaque.

Casey jumped out of the pool; water splashed on
sunbathing Peaches, who bolted for cover.
"Can you cut my hair mommy?"
"Really?"
"Yes. I want to be a boy and play baseball."
Ken, "Oh Casey, girls can play baseball.
You see mommy play."
"Then why can't I play?"
Janine, "You mean in the Pee Wee League?"
Casey nods her sad-faced head up, then down.
Ken, "Because you're not six yet."
"Oh. I have to be six."
"Yes sweetie. That's your next birthday."
"Ok, I'll stay a girl."
Casey ran back to the pool, leaped in and laid on her
stomach windmilling her arms in the water.
"Look, I'm swimming."
Peaches moved even further away.

CHAPTER FORTY-TWO

The Oasis

AKA A MILITARY COMPOUND

I was back on the road still driving north. It was all good, but man that was a ton of emotions; from spilling my story to Millie, praying with her, then calling my mom; yes, all good. I found myself exhausted. When I looked at the time I was shocked to see that it was already 8:30 at night.

I had been nibbling, driving, thinking and proffering Peaches a few treats whenever she nudged my arm. I was so lost in the impact of the day, all the days that brought me to this day, that I had forgotten the basic needs of woman and dog. We cannot live on nibbles alone.

Seeing a Rest Area sign my entire body demanded relief. Even though Peaches was sleeping, I knew that my loyal companion needed some TLC as well.

I pulled into the rest stop, not a second too soon for either girl. Once priorities were handled, I fed Peaches, then looked in the tiny fridge to see what there was to feed myself. I grab some grapes and from the cupboard a bag of mixed nuts, then sighed as the snacks found my stomach.

I had purposefully taken the semi-back roads and had no idea where I was. Perusing the large maps in the rest area I saw that I was close to

Wenatchee Washington. I didn't want to drive too much further, even with the longer summer days. As two road weary girls we were tucker out and ready to stop for the night.

"Sure. I'm with you. My love of motion has turned into motion sickness. I need out!" My furry companion confirmed my decision.

It didn't take long to be greeted by a huge sign, OASIS RV PARK, 2 Miles Ahead.

"Two miles Peaches, we are almost home."

"Petal to the medal, girl. Let's get there!" Peaches said as she twirled around in the passenger seat then stretched to look out the window. *"Are we there yet?"*

I was impressed as I pulled into the pristine, well landscaped, perfectly manicured Oasis RV Park. Suddenly feeling quite tired, I was also thankful that I would not have to go any farther. In fact, staying here for a few days, having some quiet time to sort out the impact of staying at EZ Breezee, seemed like just the thing to do.

As I got out of the van, Peaches jumped out as well. "No, no. You stay in the van." I put Peaches back inside, shut the door and turned to walk into the registration office.

The office was housed in a sweet chalet type building with window boxes that held a bright array of flowers. The flagstone walkway to the office welcomed me with rose bushes on either side, like a mega star walking along the red carpet at the Oscars. Beyond the roses was an expanse of vibrant, lush grass. I wanted to lay down on it, even in my fancy Oscar dress.

As I opened the door, the tinkling of bells announced my arrival. A stern-faced woman quickly came out from a door behind the followed by a man who I assumed was the woman's husband. Both scowled at me.

I assumed both were probably retired, since they seemed to be about the same age as George and Millie. The wife, though just a few pounds overweight, was almost as tall as me, with a long torso and short legs. The sense of height come more from the upward tilt of her nose, rather than from actual inches. It spoke, disdain.

The husband had broad shoulders, muscularly thick arms and a bearing that was military-stiff. His face was taunt and menacing. I almost shrunk back, like I had done something terribly wrong and he was about to bark an order at me.

"Um. Well, um..." Don't stammer. I encouraged myself and took a few steps toward the counter standing tall. My eyes met his, "I would like a full hook up space if there's one available."

He lifted his arm and glanced at his watch. "Nine o'clock!" he said curtly.

"Well, yes. Almost." I conceded.

"Do you always break the rules young lady?"

"Rules?"

His wife was pointing to a neatly typed, bold-lettered sign, that stated; No registrations after 9:00 p.m.

This was not going well, but I did not want to get back on the road. I stood my ground. "It's 4-minutes to nine."

Now the wife spoke, clicking her tongue, "Paperwork takes time. You don't just flit in here and expect that the world will stop for you."

I could see that the husband considered her point valid. "Mother, I think we can register this young woman; bend the rule just this once."

Humph. The woman sounded like Peaches in a snit. Then she smiled, did a complete three-sixty, "Welcome to the Oasis, let me help you get registered."

Huh. What have I gotten myself into? Can I ask for a site far, far away from where they are? I was way too worn out to hunt out another campground.

As they went through the registration process it took on military precision, even though "Mother's" tone was still friendly.

"Here dear, these are the campground rules for you to read and sign."

I glanced at the first few; check-in and check-out time, speed limit, pretty much like other campgrounds. I started to put it in my tote.

"No, no dear, you sign that copy, then I will give you a copy to keep."

Sign the rules? Oh well, I took the pen and scribbled my name.

Her husband, son? Whoever he was, stepped forward. "Did I see a dog in your van?"

"Yes. Peaches. My little Yorkie, no trouble at all."

Still smiling, Mother reached under the counter and brought out another form. "Here are the rules for pets. Please read it and sign it."

Again, I gave a quick look, noticing the standard campground restrictions; keep your pet on a leash, clean up after your pet etc. I signed that form and awaited my very own copy.

Gosh can I frame these???

"Ahem." Both of us women looked at the man, "And a bike?'

"Yes," I admitted, feeling a twinge of guilt, "I have a bike, I do a lot of cycling." And then I thought, but held my tongue. *Why? Is that a crime???*

I should have guessed, as again, Mother reached below the counter to produce yet another form, "Here are the rules for biking in the park. Please read and...."

"Yes, I know, sign it." I finished the sentence. I was tired. I just wanted to hook up and go to sleep. The woman's face tightened momentarily then she said, "Yes, dear, exactly right."

After a slew more pieces of paper and brochures crossed the counter, I was assigned a campsite. Both people behind the counter gave weak smiles and said, "Enjoy your stay at the Oasis." Mr. looked at his watch prompting me to glance at the clock. It was 9:06 p.m. I felt lucky not to be in a cell on a diet of bread and water.

I walked out, feeling their eyes piercing my back in reprimand. Maybe I was supposed to march out, not walk. Almost to the van, I saw a mailbox to the left of the walkway with the name, Miller, neatly stenciled on it.

Ok…these are the Miller's…*husband and wife or mother and son? Oh heck, who cares, I just want to sleep.*

I gave a quick tiny salute to the mailbox then, reaching the van, I opened the door, got in and locked the door. *Safe!!*

Peaches was miffed, "Sure leave me all along in a creepy place. Those roses didn't fool me."

"Believe me, you were much better off staying in the van."

I put the key in the ignition, started the van and slowly, very slowly, following Rule #4 about park speed limits, I crept along toward my site. The only utility I really needed was water, which I hooked up as Peaches, unleashed, did her final piddle of the night. Right afterwards, we both ate something a little more substantial. We curled up in bed where I read for a while to get my mind past my registration experience. I texted my family, cuddled Peaches, closed my eyes and we were fast asleep before another rule could be broken.

CHAPTER FORTY-THREE

Wrestling

WITH THE TRUTH

I was startled awake by the loud bugle-call blast of Reveille. Peaches jumped out from under the blanket. Simultaneously, I saw the time, 7:30 a.m., as I pulled back the side window curtain. I expected to see all the campers lined up for morning roll-call and calisthenics under the precise count of Sergeant Miller, "One, two. One, two. Come on, put some muscle into it. Again, one, two...."

All was quiet. Not a soul stirred. Huh? I let go of the curtain to lay back down on my pillow. I wasn't fully awake yet.

Louder. Reveille blasted again.

Quicker this time, I tore back the curtain. Just about out of sight was a kid, maybe 8-years old, riding his bike. As he turned the corner, I saw him reach out to squeeze the horn on his handlebars. Reveille.

"Ugh, there's got to be a rule against that." I thought as I gave up on sleep and worked my way out of the bed toward coffee.

Coffee. I needed coffee. First, I had to hook up the electricity and turn on the propane. I left Peaches curled up in the warm spot on the bed I had just vacated. Groggily, headed outside. In the distance I heard Reveille again, then a sharp reprimand. The young over-enthusiastic soldier had been silenced. I love rules!

Coming around to the driver's side of the van, I opened the driver's door, got out my work gloves and turned to hook up the utilities I would need. I did the electricity first, hopped back into the van, started the coffee, then went outside to finish hooking up and setting up my campsite.

There was a decent picnic table and benches on my site, but I opted for my favorite chair. As the coffee pot was doing its magic, I set up the outdoor carpet, my chair and small side table.

Perfect, I thought. I went in, poured coffee into my large mug, grabbed my journal and headed back to my outdoor living room, settling in to greet the day. I left the door open incase Peaches needed he morning piddle. But, Peaches didn't even open an eye to peek at what I was doing. A dog's life. Lucky girl.

Ah, with the comfort of my chair and coffee, I was feeling ready for a new day. No thoughts, just the stillness of morning, a few distant low voices from other camp sites. Setting my journal down, I wrapped both hands around the warm cup, lifting it toward my mouth. I stopped just before my lips; under my nose I sniffed in the deep French roast fragrance. I closed my eyes as my other senses awakened. Sips of coffee, waifs of the fragrant bean, rustle of the nearby trees, sing-song melody of birds and a surprising restfulness enveloped me.

You know I'm a planner. Usually, my mind goes into checklist mode as I detail all that I want to accomplish in the day. This morning, I did not even need to fight to keep my mind quiet. A quiet mind. I took a deep breath and expanded my diaphragm as I visualized oxygen traveling all the way into the smallest capillaries. Breathe in.... breathe out. Sip coffee. Yes.

With my eyes still closed I felt the morning sun warm my bear arms. Slowly, I lifted my eyelids as I took a long unhurried drink from my mug; coughed it out and choked back a scream.

Standing before me, near the picnic table was an enormous man, as black as the night and as big as ...as....as...an RV diesel pusher...no, a truck, an 18-wheeler. Gargantuan. He was mumbling at me, not at all lucid. As the massive insane beast peered down at me, my heart leaped into my throat. Fear coursed through my body. Strategies raced through my mind. This demanded action. Quick decisive action. Lifesaving action. *Should I scream? Oh, crumbs there's probably rules about screaming!*

As my heart rate slowed, the looming apparition made strange noises. Okay, it was not mumbling, he had some kind of thick southern accent. "You oughtin; let your little un runs free." He uttered.

Then it clicked. He wasn't human. He wasn't from the south. He was from hell. "Don't let your little one run free!" He was taunting me.

I never noticed Peaches snuggled deep within his massive arms. At his admonition I was mentally and emotionally slammed back to Dungeness and Casey. With that one statement, he ripped open a truth that I had subconsciously concealed. But he knew it. He spoke it. I couldn't hide from the truth any longer. I deserved all the punishment and retribution he would inflict upon my me.

Torrential flashes ... images of Dungeness. Forgotten words flooded over me. Impressions swallowed me. The truth screaming for acknowledge-ment.

"I did it. It was me." I wanted to confess as I remembered our campsite at Dungeness Spit. I remembered past warnings to keep my child safe.

"Don't ride in the street Casey."

"Ok Mommy."

"Where are you, Casey."

"Here Mommy." Hand waving as she tried to keep her bike steady with her other hand.

"Both hands little one. I see you."

Then images of camping that last time. Dungeness Spit. Ken chat-ting-up a couple that were camped a few sites over. Making friends. The coals have been lit. Ken is waiting for the perfect time to start cooking. We will probably have guests for dinner, if I know Ken.

I'm about to turn off Veggie Tales but am distracted watching Casey parks her bike and run inside. *"Mommy can I take Peaches out."*

"Yes Casey. Just stay between here and where Daddy is. Do you see Daddy?"

"Yes, I see him." Then she shouts, *"Hi Daddy."*

He responds, "Hi Casey." He waves both arms. He turns back to the couple. I know he will soon be telling them all about Casey and how she got her name.

Casey minds us really well. Yet like most parents we are attuned to her voice, movements and silences. Before letting her go I gave one more reminder, "Remember Casey, if a car is coming you and Peaches move to the very side of the road, stop, stand still and stay stopped until the car has gone all the way by you."

Casey stood up straighter and announced, "I know Mommy. I always do that."

"Good...good." I said smiling, then turning to head back into the trailer. I began chopping salad ingredients to the rhythm of the friendship song that was coming from the Veggie Tales DVD Casey had left playing in her rush to go outside. Added to that rhythmic chopping were my glances out the window at Casey.

I smiled; in my mind I could hear the voice of my daughter singing along with every Veggie Tale song. How did she know all the words? It astounded me. Casey loved music, could hear a song once and was able to sing it from then on, in her sweet little six-year-old voice.

Little did I know that an older couple, Felix and Sofia had checked into the park and had begun to follow the campground map to their site.

"Turn there dear, Spring Lane." Sofia, the chief navigator, directed.

"Got it. We're almost home." Felix responded, tired but alert as he maneuvered the park road.

Sofia knew a long day of travel wore them both out. They would have arrived earlier and fresher had they not missed the turn off to the campground. They were miles beyond their destination when they realized they were lost. Then they had to try to find a place to turn their rig around on a narrow country road. Not an easy feat as they looked for a turn off or wider section in the road.

Assuring Felix that they were almost done for the day Sofia said, "I'm ready for dinner. There's a tasty casserole that I'll heat up and a nice glass of wine. Wine and casserole. We going upscale." Sofia said fluffing her hair for effect.

Casey did what she was taught the minute she saw the truck pulling the rig. She moved tight again a group of trees, stopped and stood to wait. Ken caught Casey standing like a soldier against the row of trees, a good distance from the oncoming truck. He judged that she was safely to the side of the road and turned back to his new friends to wrap up their chap and head over to Casey. He was proud that Casey was full of life but also well behaved when it came to following Janine and his guidance.

Unfortunately, Ken didn't see Peaches get loose or Felix's flawed maneuvering skills.

Felix's far-reaching truck with its attached fifth-wheel made Casey stretch her neck to see to the end. It never ended. It reminded her of waiting, in their stopped car, at a train crossing. She was mesmerized by the rhythmic, click-click, click-click, as more and more train cars rattled past. She always wondered if it would ever end.

Although this very long house-on-wheels fascinated her, she stood very still, until Peaches bolted. Ken had already turned back to quickly invite the couple to dinner then go stand with Casey. He felt assured that all was well and didn't see Casey instinctively as she began to run after Peaches. Simultaneously, Felix made an error in judgement. It all happened in an instant.

Towing their 37' fifth wheel, Felix began to make the tight turn down the narrow packed-gravel road toward their site. They made the mistake so many others make when hauling larger rigs. They did not swing out far enough to account for the arc of the rig and that the rear of the fifth wheel extended far beyond its dual wheels.

Casey did not see the final turn of the fifth wheel when the tail end swung way out past its wheelbase and headed toward her. Even if she had seen it, with trees right behind her, there was no place for her to go. One instant she was an innocent little girl humming to herself as she patiently stood by the trees. The next, she took a few steps to run after Peaches. The tail end of Felix's trailer hit her and pushed her with a tremendous force, back against a tree.

Janine was bombard with this horrific memory when her immense tormentor spoke those piercing words, "You oughtin; let your little un runs free."

She dropped her coffee cup and fled into her van, slamming the door and locking it before throwing herself on the bed. The man stood in place as he watched the young woman, terror pouring out from her eyes, run into her van. Then he heard her muffled screams.

Oh Mommy...do you hear all the music.
Voices. So many voices, singing.
It sounds like the Christmas music at church when
everyone is singing. Only this is better.
It's soooo pretty Mommy.

CHAPTER FORTY-FIVE

Wrapped

IN LOVE

Janine's flashbacks to that day continued.

Casey never heard the piercing sound that echoed throughout the campground when the RV's tail end collided with the tree. Everyone else did. At the neighbor's campsite, Ken was closest to the cab of Felix's truck, so he was the first to respond. He did not yet comprehend Casey's proximity to the fifth wheel's impact. He just wanted to stop the elderly driver before any more damage could be done to the fifth wheel.

He threw both hands up, palms pressing toward the cab, motioning to the driver to stop. Stop. Felix had felt the jolt of contact with the tree and was already applying his brakes as Sofia too was shouting, "Stop. Felix. Stop,"

People from other camp sites were coming to watch Ken help another RVer out of a jam, some ready to chime in with their expertise. I, as well, came out of the trailer, having heard the horrible screech even over the Veggie Tales music.

With the truck stopped Ken went to assess the damage so he could help the driver correct his position. I became anxious at not seeing Casey and called out to Ken, "Where's Casey?"

Ken could not hear me over the loud rumble of Felix's diesel engine. Meanwhile Felix had thrown the truck into park and got out to look at what happened and to see how his turn went wrong so he could correct his mistake.

Both men, Ken and Felix, got to the tail end about the same time. Both were distracted by the escalation of voices of people at the other side of the fifth wheel, people who could see exactly what had happened. Unable to sort out what was being said, Ken and Felix simultaneously looked to where the people were pointing.

I was walking fast toward Ken shouting, "Where's Casey, Ken? Do you see Casey?"

Others saw her. That part of her not concealed by the fifth wheel. It took a few seconds to register what they were seeing.

The cries. The anguish. The screams of denial. People. Shouting. Clawing. Reaching. Fighting to release Casey, reverberated through every single person there.

Parents took their children away from experiencing a gruesome reality. A woman wrapped her arms around me and gently pulled me away. I tried to fight her but realized I couldn't. Men and women came together trying with all their will, to lift the trailer. Felix jumped back into the truck and slowly moved it forward.

Ken reached around for Casey, while someone motioned to Felix with his arm saying, "Yes. Forward. Careful...careful..."

A momentary sense of pain, a soft whimper.
Then it was over.
She opened her eyes. He was standing very near to her.
Though she had never met him before she knew him.
"Hi." She said, as if to her best friend Gina.
He responded with a kind, welcoming smile.
She felt a rush of love wash over her, the way it felt when
Daddy tucked her in bed at night, then snuggled with her.
"Am I going with you?"
"I have a special place for you, little one."
She glanced back at her parents; He understood
her unspoken concern and assured her,
"They'll be along soon."
"Mommy and daddy are crying."
"I will catch every teardrop that falls."
She nodded, placed her small hand in his.
"Yes, Jesus loves me."
Glowing, feather-soft beings floated all
around them smiling and singing.

CHAPTER FORTY-SEVEN

We Knew

It took less than a foot of the truck moving the RV forward to free Casey. Ken, who had moved in closer as the RV slowly separated from the tree, caught Casey as she was released from being pinned. She was a collapsed bundle in his arms, just like she was whenever she fell asleep in the car. Ken would open the back door, wrap one arm behind her, undo the seatbelt and Casey would fall like a ragdoll, his little doll, into Ken's arms.

Squatted down, he held his sleeping little girl, his Casey in a gentle embrace. She looked so peaceful; he almost convinced himself that she truly was just sleeping after a long day on the road.

Felix got back out of his truck and motioned for people to give Ken room, to stand back. Ken looked over and saw me, my back to him, being comforted by a woman. He nodded to the woman who then started walking, leading me over to Ken and Casey.

Ken saw my eyes as I saw Casey and I knew she was gone. Then he too knew. The knowing was too much for us. Tears. Pleadings. Moans. Wails. Fist pounding.

Time stopped. Life stopped. For all three of us.

Chapter Forty-Eight

Fines

and Broken Rules

That day at the Oasis RV campground condemning words were mumbled at me. All of what happened at Dungeness, every single second, became a deluge gushing through my body because a mammoth black apparition looked straight into my soul and compelled me to see the horror of it all. I could not hide anymore.

I was guilty. I let Casey die. I found myself inside my van, screaming into my pillow, slamming my fists against the bed. I was spent. Nothing was left within me as my arms stopped pounding, my sobs subsided, and I waited for my breathing to slow down.

As if returning from some far-off place, I rolled over and lethargically sat up. I recoiled and let out a muted yelp. Out my privacy blinds I could make out the immense form of my accuser. He was right where I had first seen him, arms still casually crossed, looking down; still mumbling. I couldn't take it anymore. He had to leave; I had to get rid of him.

With resolve, that I didn't really feel, I walked to the front of my van, reached for the pepper spray and prepared to face down the embodiment of my remorse and guilt.

Harley hadn't moved. He had heard Janine's screams. He was familiar with the sounds of a tormented soul. He had heard the sounds all too often; of pain so bottomless that once it begins to find an expression it thunders with such an unearthly reverberation that mountains quake. Anguish. Heartache. Woeful misery.

He did the only thing he knew to do; what he had learned to do, out of his own desperation. He looked up, then, in reverence, he looked down and began to pray for the young woman, me, who had run from him into the van.

I stepped out of my camper, my arm straight forward, pointing the pepper spray at the manifestation that stood a few yards from me. If he speaks again I will nihilate him. Tough words, as my hands shook.

He raised his head and whispered, "I'm big. Scares som' peoples. I mean no harm. Jes' wanna give your lit'l one back to ya fer there's any problem. Tha's all."

He uncrossed one arm and wrapped his huge hand around something tiny in the crook of his other arm. Peaches.

"Peaches?"

Peaches wiggled awake and peered over her keeper's thumb at me. *"Yes girl, it's me. And I was having a really good dream. You really must try to respect a lady's nap time."*

"Peaches?" He asked nodding down at the bundle in his hand. He saw my entire countenance relax, so he took a step toward me with his hand holding Peaches out in front of him; a peace offering.

"Sorry I did scare ya. Name's Harley."

"Oh, um...yes. Sorry 'bout that. I thought you said. Well, I mean. Just sorry, ok?" Gaining some sense of normalcy, I put the pepper spray in my pocket and extended my hands to receive Peaches, "I'm Janine."

"Janine." Softly, he tried out my name, "Don't mean to be a both'r. Jest that, the rules. Ya gots to follow all dem rules or the militants will fine ya."

"The militants?"

"Heh, heh." Harley laughed, his whole-body taking part in the joviality, registering a 6.0 on the Richter scale. "That be my name for them Millers. The miller-tants! E'vry ting has a rule. E'vry rule gots money to be paid if ya breaks it."

"The militants." I tried to laugh; it was perfectly descriptive. Not quite relaxed, the laugh sounded forced to me so I said, "That's a good one."

Something was drawing me to Harley, a curiosity, so I kept the chatter going, "I know, they handed me a bunch of papers to sign with "THE RULES." But I don't remember fines that had to be paid. Then again, it was late and I was tired."

"Pet off iz leash, $10. Second time, $25. Din't want you to pay for that lil un." Harley explained pointing at Peaches, now held in my arms peering around as we conversed.

"I didn't even know she was out. I left her sound asleep in the van while I was doing the hook ups. The little escape artist snuck out when I wasn't looking. Thanks for catching her. Oh, and saving me $10."

"Yo surely are welcome. Now I be gettin m'self to work. Stop on o'er the Big Easy for a little Cajun eatin' if ya like." Harley petted Peaches then headed to the park exit.

"Uh, Thanks Harley." I said as he turned and walked beyond my view. I stared at the vacated place where Harley had stood, dumbfounded. *What just happened?*

I had no words. I had no brain cells to form words. I took Peaches into the camper, put her down by her food bowl, grabbed an energy bar and a bottle of water, and then sat down on my bed. Peaches quickly followed, curled up and went in search of the wonderful dream that had been stolen from her earlier.

I nibbled, drank and didn't think, though I did feel lighter having been pushed to face what I had kept stuffed down deep inside. It was out. Remembering had felt like being ripped apart. Yet here I was. I even laughed, well almost. And I lived. It felt like I had walked out of a horror movie into a bright day where the earlier darkness had been dissipated by the sun's rays.

A few moments later, I grabbed my book and went outside to read, closing the door securely.

CHAPTER FORTY-NINE

Recovery

Reading had led to me dozing in my chair. Opening my eyes, I felt rested but still a bit wrung out; recovery mode, like what I used to feel after working out hard at the gym. This was more than just my body in recovery, it was my mind and heart as well. Having always been an active person, rarely sitting still, I had to tell myself that this slo-mo mode was part of healing, something to be expected. *Think of a broken leg, The cast that is a constant reminder that healing took time. This need for rest is the cast around my heart as I heal.*

I didn't fight it. Rest was my first response, and the brief nap helped. Next was a nice high-protein, light lunch. I made myself an egg and cheese wrap, a tall glass of water [no ice] and half of a crisp, sweet apple. I gladly shared my apple with Peaches who would be a vegetarian except she liked to nibble on shrimp as well.

"It keeps my coat shinny." Was Peaches explanation, as she wagged her tail and tilted her head up for another bite from the apple.

With my stomach satisfied yet not stuffed, I knew what was needed for the remainder of the day. Nothing. Do absolutely nothing. No "to do" list, no cycling, sprucing up, exploring, just nothing. The only way I could do nothing was to continue reading. Beside the Clive Cussler book was moving fast and I knew the adventurers needed my help to survive.

I loved to read. Earlier I had l lifted the top off the tote under my bed. I swooned over the choices I had stowed away for myself, Clive, Vince, Parker, Brad...thrills, adventure, stealth, good clean fun, excitement and nail-biting times awaited me. Oh, which one to choose? I finally reached in and grabbed one. Clive Cussler's Oregon File series. I was ready for the heroics of Dirk, Juan and his team. My own adventures, if you could call them that, were little too raw for me.

I topped off my water and went outside. After positioning my chair to catch the warmth of the sun but avoid the glare on the pages of my book, I called out to Peaches who immediately hopped down the step and up onto my lap. Whoops, this reminded me that I had, once again left the door open. Bad habit. Remembering this morning's lesson about the rules and the cost of breaking them, I held onto Peaches, got up, reached into the RV for the leash, then sat back down, attaching the leash to Peaches and wrapping it around the arm of my chair.

I waited a moment expecting Peaches to rebel or at least speak her mind, instead, my little buddy settled into my lap with her tiny back curled into my stomach. I petted Peaches for a few minutes, sipping my water and soaking in the leisure of the day. I opened my book ready to be of service, to give advice or cheer on the crew in their escapades.

CHAPTER FIFTY

Celebrating Six

Felix and Sofia were about to have a fight. Not a little spat that ends with a smile and quick "sorry." Not a tiff that ends up as a joke where they both laugh at the silliness of it all. No, not even a kiss was going to remedy the tension that had been building all morning.

Felix didn't know it was coming. Sofia knew. She was fed up with his behavior and wanted an answer once and for all.

"I can't believe you scheduled a workshop for that day, of all days." She said sharply.

Felix just looked at her like he didn't understand why that was such a problem. Yet he knew. In fact, he had scheduled the workshop purposely to avoid having to attend the birthday party that was sure to be held on that same day.

"Felix don't ignore me. What's going on?"

"Nothing. I just thought it would be good for the community pastors to meet again, like we have been, quarterly [he emphasized it with lame reasoning] and discuss a few things, plan, encourage one another…"

"Oh don't. Don't. You know what I mean. Why THAT Saturday. It's Lydia's birthday party."

"Oh...um, guess I didn't realize." Felix was usually so forthcoming, yet here he was tap-dancing around the issue. "Sorry. Lydia will have so much fun with her little friends; she won't miss me."

"That's not it, Felix. Not at all. There's something more going on and I want you to help me understand what that something is!"

"Sofia...really, it's just one party. In a few years, Lydia won't even remember that I wasn't there."

"She will remember all the other times." Sofia pushed back emphatically, "Like for this past year or so, all the times we went to visit or stopped by. She ran up to you for a hug and some Gramps time."

"She always hugged me."

Sofia wanted to scream. Felix had always treated their youngest grandchild with distance. Sure, he would hug her, obligatorily, leaving Lydia confused and yearning for more.

Fuming at her husband's avoidance tactics, Sofia tried to keep her voice as calm as possible, which was a bit on edge "What is it? Felix? I know you were upset when Geoffrey told us he and Elena were getting a divorce...."

"We both were." He reminded me, "Divorce hurts too many people. We raised Geoff to know that too. And what about their kids. My heart broke for the kids, as yours did."

"Yes, but we said our piece to Geoff and agreed to support him, Elena and the kids as best we could through it all. Spill, what is it? Is it because he got remarried? Was it that Raylene is fifteen years younger than him? Or that he and Raylene started a family and had Lydia? You know Geoff takes care of all his kids."

"He sure did rush into another marriage. And Raylene was pretty young." Felix agreed, "But really Sofia, I am fine with it all. Even Elena has remarried. I can accept all of that. There is no problem."

Sofia felt put off, like Felix was still avoiding the core issue. She had seen him time and again when they visited Geoff and Raylene. After he gave Lydia the perfunctory hug, he would find an excuse to do something else.

Watch the game on TV, help Geoff in the shop, walk the dog. He was such a wonderful Dad; Sofia had always known he would carry that into grand parenting. Actually, he had with all the other grandkids. But not so with Lydia recently.

Was he not admitting that he was still disappointed with Geoff leaving Elena? Or was it, Raylene. He was distant at first but now seemed to embrace her as part of the family. For too long now there was a barrier between Lydia and her Gramps that was all from Felix. His actions broke Sofia's heart each time she saw her little granddaughter look up at Gramps, to follow him around, only to be shooed off or gently dismissed.

"Felix you are frustrating me to no end. I just can't make sense of this." Her voice was rising. No matter what she tried she could not get an acceptable answer out of him. He kept avoiding the obvious and for the life of her, Sofia could not discern what was eating at him.

She stomped out of the kitchen in a huff making sure Felix heard the exasperation in each word. Stomping didn't help. Stomping only escalated her vexation. She stormed back into the kitchen to see Felix calmly pouring another cup of coffee. Now she was really infuriated, and he would know it!

"Basta ya de esta locura. No sé qué está pasando y seguramente no quieres contármelo. Así que, esto es lo que hay, Quiero que canceles ese taller para pastores. Punto. ¡Y final de la discusión!" [*Just stop this craziness. I don't know what is going on and you surely don't seem willing to tell me. So, this is it. I want you to cancel that pastors' workshop. Period. End of discussion!*]

Felix put down his coffee and turned to face Sofia. When she reverted to Spanish he knew he was in deep trouble.

Sofia was in rare form; she felt he had it coming. She continued, "You are going to the birthday party. You know how fast times flies. These are special family moments. No two ways about it."

"I...don't know. I...it's all planned, mi amor."

"They all have kids even grandkids. They know all about family." Sofia was not going to give in this time. She continued, "Well, darn it. Just tell them it is Lydia's sixth birthday."

Sofia swallowed the rest of her tirade when she saw Felix expression contort and he turned from her just as his eyes welled up with tears.

"Sixth. Six years old." She repeated, stunned as the truth sank in and Sofia knew. That niggling in the back of her mind, that persistent nudging that never seemed to produce an answer finally sprung forth with clarity. She got it. She knew what pain Felix was trying to avoid, thought he was avoiding the pain by unconsciously keeping Lydia at arm's length.

In that instant Felix's action started to make sense. Lydia, their darling little granddaughter, was the only girl in their family of all the kids and grandkids. There's something about little girls that urge parents and grandparents to protect them. How had I not put this together before?

Sofia whispered, knowing that the dreadful accident at Dungeness lived with them always. "Is this about Casey?" She was six when the accident happened.

Felix just stared at Sofia not wanting to go there. Not wanting to admit the self-punishing actions that he had inflicted upon himself every time he was near Lydia.

After a while he nodded yes. "Our two kids were boys. The three grandkids are all boys. Then we have this sweet, bubbly little girl, Lydia added to our family." Felix choked back a sob. "Since last summer, I have felt that I have no right to love her. And if I love her too much, will she be taken from us for what I did?'

Tears escaped his eyes streaking his cheeks and dropping onto his shirt.

Sofia was overcome by the words pouring from Felix, like a wound being lanced to remove a gangrenous infection; the realization of what Felix believed in his heart was not pretty. She walked over to face Felix and took his hands in hers.

He could barely speak as he choked on his tears, "Every time I look at Lydia I am stabbed in the heart. Ken and Janine can't cuddle Casey. They can't sing to her or wrestle with her or play Candyland. All the things I long to do with Lydia. I just can't. I am not trying to ignore or hurt Lydia. It just doesn't seem right to be so in love with a little girl when I stole someone else's darling child."

Sofia stood wordless, just listening as Felix articulated all the pent-up self-recriminations. He was a pastor. His entire life was spent in ministry sharing God's love, grace, truth and forgiveness. How did he not accept from God what he so often offered to others? He had preached all those words of forgiveness, that there is no condemnation in Christ, that God is the redeemer of our lives. He had counseled many with those beliefs for years. What could Sofia say that would even begin to reach the depth of his despair; a despair that made him forget all that Christ can do for him.

They had been standing in the kitchen. Sofia led Felix to his favorite chair in the family room and pulled over a side chair to sit next him, taking his hands once more in hers. Silently, she prayed, *"Oh Lord, only you can speak to the innermost part of Felix's torment heart. Help him feel true forgiveness; the forgiveness that you have allowed him to bring to others in your name. He needs to know it is for himself."*

When Sofia ran out of words, she was quiet for a while; then she raised her head and met Felix's eyes. "I didn't know I was holding onto all of that." He paused reflecting on what he had just verbalized. With his voice still shaky he said, "It seems I have some personal inventory to work through with God." He tried to smile; it was a weak attempt that fell from his face instantly releasing more tears.

Sofia could find no words to respond. Felix, finally able to speak, said, "This won't be easy. No quick fix. I've been holding all this in, and it has affected my actions. I wasn't even truly conscious of what I had been doing."

Sofia nodded in affirmation.

Felix reached out and brought Sofia onto his lap, holding her as his lifeline, so thankful for her insistence that he be honest with her; honest with himself. Just articulating the thoughts and seeing the self-punishment he had assigned to himself; that he had buried within his daily life, was a release.

He loved Lydia. She was his delight. She woke up the deadest parts of him. Yet he had repeatedly denied himself that joy, believing he was so unworthy of her innocent beaming love.

When had he stopped accepting God's forgiveness? When had he not allowed Lydia to be fully alive in his life to make up for Casey's lack of life? Did that balance any scales; there weren't any scales. Life never played out that way. Fair. Even. Always balanced. No, that wasn't how life went. Why did he hold himself in contempt when even God did not, the maker of Heaven and Earth?

And what about Lydia? In his selfish absorption, in his denial of her radiant joy, in his rejection of allowing himself to embrace his dear precious grandchild, he had abandoned and rebuffed her, his sweet Lydia.

"Oh Sofia." He murmured, holding her tightly to his chest, his heart, "Thank you mi amor. Thank you."

They embraced each other for quite a while. The sun had moved around their house and shined in through the window directly onto them. Felix started to raise them both up. He needed to move, shake off the barnacles of grief that had hung heavily on him. "Let's take a walk and enjoy the sun's soothing warmth."

"What a wonderful idea. Want to take along a mug of chamomile tea?"

"Yes. Sun and tea, to warm our souls." Felix said as he stretched his arms and shifted his body to awaken his old bones.

They walked in silence, stopping to absorb the sun and sip their tea heading toward downtown, just five blocks from their condo. Instinctively, they both headed in the same direction toward their favorite bench, perfect for catching the late morning sunshine.

Sitting there several neighbors and friends stopped to chat. About an hour later Felix said, "Shall we head home."

"Yes. I am ready to have some of that chicken pasta salad I made last night for lunch. How 'bout you?"

"Oh yes. I can taste it now."

It wasn't until they were a block from home that Felix wrapped up the thoughts that had been running through his mind.

"I think this morning loosened a mighty boulder that created a wall, blocking my heart. I don't want to have that kind of hardness undermine my life, our lives, Lydia's life, ever again. I think I'll set up an appointment to talk with Don, seek his Godly counsel."

Sofia silently thanked God for Felix's decision, "He has always given you wise counsel in the past. I think that's a good idea."

Felix was in awe at how God worked. Today was just another day, until Sofia got riled up and picked a fight. He passively tried to avoid her jabs but that only made her angrier. It was the onslaught of all her feelings and observations that grabbed at his heart and shook loose what he had kept stuffed down for all these months. He had been shocked as he listened to his own words of reproach and realized the conflicting signals he had been giving little Lydia. Never again.

"And yes, I will set another date for the pastors to meet. Lydia is going to get all of her Gramps for her sixth birthday. She shouldn't suffer for the accident I caused. And I need to stop punishing myself which will allow me to pour lots of love on that little sweetheart."

CHAPTER FIFTY-ONE

Cajun Style

I had gotten quickly absorbed in the good storytelling as I read late into the afternoon, sipping my water, petting Peaches who slept soundly in my lap. I hadn't even noticed the tension slowly shedding from me, like Peaches in the summer. Tension and hair falling to the ground. It was subtle but quietly liberating. I had even taken a gentle walk as opposed to my long strides as I did a cardio workout.

A slight breeze and the murmur of voices made me look up. Cars holding families and groups of people were making their way back toward campsites after their outings of the day. Unloading kids, coolers and supplies; dogs bounded from cars, owners caught them to put them on leashes [thereby avoiding fines]; parents gave instructions, a couple unhitched their bikes, two young men lifted a kayak off the top of their car. A few new campers setting up for their stay completed the campground experience, that of people watching.

I sighed, remembering our family's bustling activities. Those times felt like a lifetime ago. Now, I sat, happy to have had a quiet day to read; just sit. Life had changed me from the always-on-the go, there's lots to do and see person I used to be. You didn't know me then. Today, I found contentment in reading a book with nature wrapped around me.

The deep rumbling bark of a Lab brought Peaches awake.

"Huh. What???" A startled Peaches looked up at me.

"How 'bout a little walk girl. You know, take care of business."

Peaches squirmed, *"Just unchain me and let me handle this on my own."*

"No, no. You can't afford the fine." I said as I set Peaches on the ground, then stood and stretched, careful to hold onto her leash. Sure enough, patrolling the lively commotion of returning campers were the Millers. He, standing tall, walking long-legged yet stiffly, she, on shorter legs, taking two steps to his one long stride. Both nodded curtly but not stopping to chat, eyes alert to any rule-breaking or limit-pushing acts. Their almost-scowling faces said it all; *"We're watching you, you untrustworthy transients. You can't fool us."*

"Makes you want to stand at attention while we are inspected doesn't it Peaches?" I commented and then heard a chuckle behind me.

"Sure does." A woman who was just walking her bike past my site responded. Her smile halted any embarrassment I almost felt at talking out loud to a dog.

"I'm Phyllis." She said, balancing her bike against her hip as she reached out her hand in greeting.

I responded in kind, shaking Phyllis's hand, "Janine." Nodding downward, "and Peaches. Who needs a tree fairly quickly."

"Oh, then don't let me hold you up. I see you have a road bike. I'm at site G16 if you want to know about some good biking routes."

"Thanks. I do. I'll stop by." I said as Peaches began tugging at the leash, well tugging would be too strong of a feat for Peaches, but she made her needs known. I jogged toward some bushes and a few trees, in the opposite direction of the Millers. I glanced over my shoulder as Peaches squatted wondering, *Is there a fine for piddling?*

I circled around the campground to give Peaches a little walk and, truth be told, to avoid the Millers. I found myself in the 'G' section, so I looked for #16. There was Phyllis cleaning off her bike and oiling the chain.

"Hi." I called out as I approached. "You take good care of your bike."

Phyllis looked up, "Thanks to friends who beat into me the importance of proper bike maintenance. They put me through bike-care boot camp! Not only can I clean my bike, I can repair any mishap along the road. They were merciless. Grueling. But I wouldn't have had it any other way. What about you? I noticed you have a Trek road bike; do you do long distance cycling?"

"Use to but not lately. I've started doing more and got up to about 30 miles a few times over the last few weeks. Not the 75-100 I used to do."

"That's a good start." Phyllis stood up and reached into her front pack to get out a map. "Let me show you where I rode today. It was about 35 miles. I could have gone further, but I did a long ride two days ago, so I just wanted to stay in motion without pushing myself."

"I know what you mean."

Phyllis re-traced her route giving me a running dialog of the terrain, elevation gain and bike-friendliness of the roads. "Overall I think this area is welcoming to cyclists." She said as she began to fold up the map. "I keep thinking I will get a holder for my phone and use its map, but there's something about paper for me."

With anticipation Janine asked, "Will you be riding tomorrow?"

"Probably so, wanna come along? I'm fine with whatever type of ride you want to do."

The thought of riding with someone and tackling a route she'd never ridden before thrilled her, "Sure. That would be great. Is there a route that gives us options as to how far we go? We could start with a goal of 30 but I'd like to do 50 miles, if I can."

"Oh, I'm sure there is. Let's check out the map." She re-opened the map, laid it on the picnic table, and we began to searching for the best route to ride.

"Mind if I invite a few friends along for the ride?" Phyllis asked.

"Sure, if they can put up with an out-of-shape rider."

"We've all been there. This is a great bunch of riders. We were actually part of the Half America Cycling Tour. It was an assisted ride. We didn't have to be self-contained, carrying all our gear and preparing all our food. They had several large trucks that carried our gear, a bunch of spotter vans, in case anyone needed aid, and at the end of the day a catering truck made us dinner. Oh, and a nice breakfast to get us started each day. All we had to do was ride and enjoy the view."

"Sounds like a nice trip. Where did you finish?"

"We never did finish. Well, a few of us didn't finish. When we hit Utah and Arches National Park, we knew we wanted to do more than eat, ride, sleep, and ride some more. We wanted time to explore and play. Even though we paid for the full deal, we went AWOL. Well, kind of, we did tell the team leaders we were going out on our own. They weren't happy with our decision after all, they do a lot to put these rides together. But we left on friendly terms."

"Renegades, huh?"

"Yup. But we've had a blast. One of the unofficial support team members was the wife of a rider you'll meet. She now carries all our gear in her SUV and even makes us dinner after we've been riding. We've been here a week and love it. Our plan is to stay a bit longer. We're thinking of creating a ride and hike trip that includes some interesting parks we noticed."

"Are you sure I will fit in? I have only been back riding for the past few weeks. It has been a while since I rode any distance. I mean, I think I can do it but I am a bit rusty."

"Hey to us it's about the camaraderie. We just enjoy being out on our bikes. No pressure to perform. You'll be just fine. That was another reason we left the group. There was always a subtle undercurrent to perform, compete, to out ride what you did the day before or the person ahead of you. We just wanted to enjoy the world around us."

"Okay you sold me, I'm definitely in."

Peaches, still annoyingly tethered to her leash, found a patch of sun and was absorbing as much of the rays as possible by laying on her tummy with her legs stretched out. Cycling held no interest to her whatsoever. *I mean, get a clue, I can't reach the peddles!*

Phyliss took out a highlighter from her pack and showed Janine the route they would try the next day with options to shorten the route, if needed.

"That looks like a challenging route, but I'm ready for some exertion. Well, guess I'd better get Peaches fed and heat up some leftovers for my dinner."

Phyllis bent down to acknowledge Peaches, "Cute dog. Bet she's good company."

"She keeps me in line." I smiled at the absurdity of my statement. With a yip, Peaches stood up and assured Phyllis that she did indeed keep me on the straight and narrow.

Seeing Peaches ears perk up Phyllis asked, "Is your dog talking?"

"She's bi-lingual, sometimes she mews." I smiled. "Well, see ya tomorrow, seven a.m., right?"

"Hey wait. You mention dinner. Have you ever eaten at the Big Easy?"

"You mean where Harley works?" I hadn't given Harley's invitation any further thought. I didn't want to interrupt someone while they were working.

"Well, he does a little more than work there, but yeh. The food's really good. I'm heading over there with a few of the cycling crew. Why don't you join us? You can get to know this crazy bunch before heading out in the morning."

I was about to find an excuse not to go along but I'd already had plenty of 'alone' time. Interacting with others would be exhilarating. I didn't want to share my life story but then again, I liked Phyllis, we had riding in common. Sure, why not.

"Sure. Sounds like a better plan than I had. In fact, I don't even know what I was going to find in the fridge."

"Great. Give me, let's say, an hour. Then we'll head over. I'll come by your camper with Ryan, Pete, Colleen and Gary."

Real people, with names. I'm ready for this! "See you in an hour." I said as I turned back toward my site.

I fed Peaches, washed my face, changed clothes and then texted my aunt, parents and my brother Danny.

"I'm near Wenatchee. Met a few cyclists so we're going out to eat. All is well. Hope so with you too. Love and hugs."

With nothing left to do but wait, I began to pace the five feet of walking area in my camper letting my nerves get the best of me.

I could leave a note on my door saying I didn't feel well. If I had gotten Phyllis's cell number, I could have texted her. What was I thinking? There will be questions. Where are you from Janine? What do you do? Going to Washington huh, any place special? You're from Washington, how'd you end up in Arizona?

Nope. No. Nada. I couldn't do it. I wasn't ready. Too many questions. No good answers. I rummaged through my junk drawer and found a black maker; ripped out a blank page form my journal and began to write my excuse.

Tape. I need a piece of tape. No tape.

I'll slide the note partially under the lip of the little window on the camper door that should hold it but keep it visible. My stomach was growling, hunger, nerves. It didn't really matter which, I just knew I was not ready for people.

Heading toward the camper door, I closed the mini blinds on each window so I could hide out, sight unseen. I stood still as the world within the womb of my camper dimmed. In here I felt safe, secure, protected, and hidden from intruding questions.

Voices. Sounds. A light knock.

"Hey Janine, you ready?" Phyllis' voice.

No.

I.

Am.

Not.

Ready.

Go away.

Didn't I do this at my aunt's house, hide away? I'm not going back into a shell. I'm ready to live. Get out there, do normal activities. Meet people.

My little pep talk worked. I crumbled my note, threw it on the bed, got my purse and opened the door.

"Guess so." I said. Here's to an evening that included socializing with real live people. I used to be drawn to people, groups and fun gathering, the extroverted life of any party. To put on my "forward moving" mind set, I quipped, "My stomach says I'm ready."

"Mine too. Hey, this is Colleen who's married to Gary, and this is my brother Ryan and our fix-it guy Pete. We all go to the State University in Utah together. Colleen drives the SUV and is our support." Turning to Colleen she quipped, "Tonight is your night off, no meal prep, we're buying you dinner!"

Hellos abounded as everyone greeted me. Or conversation quickly centered on common ground, asking about my cycling and sharing their stories. They moved as one toward the front of the campground and headed down a few short blocks to the historic downtown. The Big Easy was about three-quarters of the way into the heart of town. An easy walk from the campground.

As we approached, the group remembered their commonality, hunger.

"What was that sausage dish you got last time Phyliss?" Ryan asked his sister.

"You mean the sausage and eggplant. The spices made it taste a bit Italian but with a Cajun kick. You had that Hoppin' Harley rice plate right Pete?" Phyliss asked.

"Whoa Nelly, was that ever hot with cut up jalapeno and sausage over some southern pea and rice concoction." He exclaimed. "I couldn't get enough. It took a lot of beer to smother that four-alarm fire in my mouth"

"Any excuse for another brew." Gary joked.

"I like a little heat but that sounds volcanic." Ryan said to Pete.

My mouth was watering as I thought about the new foods I would try. "This will be my first time eating Cajun food. I barely knew the word until I met Harley just this morning."

"Harley's the best. He'll know just how to get you started."

I still didn't know exactly what Harley did at the restaurant and was again concerned about interrupting him at work. Then again, if he were a waiter, that could work out okay.

"What does Harley do? Wait tables?"

"Well, sure, you could say that." Phyllis said as Ryan opened the door to the Big Easy and we filed into a loud, uproarious room overflowing with people. People weren't just sitting at tables nicely set apart from other patrons. There were clusters of tables that had been pulled together. People moved from one group to the other or drew their table over to another table. They were shouting and talking across the crowd. In the middle of it all, bigger than life [and Mount Everest] was Harley. Waiting tables. Clinking beer bottles with customers. Laughing and shouting out food orders.

Phyllis was laughing at my shocked expression, "Welcome to the Big Easy. No rules here. I bet the Millers drive miles out of their way to avoid this place."

Colleen added, "It's just one big happy family. The minute you enter you've joined the family. Reminds me of the back streets of Little Italy in New York."

Gary agreed, "Exactly. No goombahs' but lots of noise. Hey there's a table, let's grab it." He pointed and led the way.

The controlled bedlam continued as we wove our way to a table which almost touched the one next to it. "Hey, hi." The neighboring patrons said as we were getting settled.

"Hi backatcha." Ryan said, extending his arm to shake hands. "I'm Ryan, this is Colleen, Phyllis, Gary, Pete and...."

"Janine. I'm Janine."

"That's it. Janine. We picked her up on the way over." Ryan said grinning.

Ryan had just sat down, when that southern booming voice rose above all the other voices, "Well, well, Lordy, Lordy, take my heart...looky who be comin' here y'all."

The crowd parted as Harley made his way toward our table. "My tru luv. She sure be my life, my breath...Janine!" He exclaimed with a huge grin, one enormous hand over his heart and the other reaching out toward me.

At the sound of my name I froze, the words registering amid all the commotion around me. I turned away from the big voice as if looking at someone. I wanted to hide the expression on my face. *His own true love. What. Where did he get that idea?*

The morning's encounter rushed through my mind's eye as I tried to remember what I said that could have misled this grizzly bear of a man making his way toward us. Towards me!

"I knew you'd be comin'...knew'd we had a thing. I be so irresistible right? Love at first sight of big ole me. Smack. It hit you and here we be. Just right in love we bof be."

I felt my heart flutter. Not in love but in desperation. Harley was a nice guy but his effervescent love? Where'd that come from? What signals had he misinterpreted?

Now the entire swell of human beings was all turned in my direction; some were cheering, a mellow tenor voice began singing an old sappy love song.

Harley put down the order he held in one hand, stretched his arms wide above everyone as he continued making his way to me. I glanced at his approach, then looked at Phyllis who was grinning and doing all she could to hold back busting out into full blown laughter.

When she saw the panic on my face, she recognized something deeper than just confusion. Her laughter instantly became compassion. "Janine, it's ok. Harley greets all newcomers this way. He just loves the Big Easy and everyone who comes in to share it with him... everyone is his own true love."

As Phyllis' words penetrated my shocked mind, blood began to flow again through my body. My face relaxed and within a moment I too could accept this gentle goliath who was so totally in love with me he was shouting it to the rooftops.

Harley had reached our table. The crowd fully caught up in the theatrics as Harley went down on one knee, his hands outstretched imploring me to take hold.

"Sorry Harley." I said, finally able to join in with the performance, "My heart belongs to another. Peaches."

"Y'all meanin' that mangy wild beast you be callin' a dog?"

"True Harley."

And the entire crowd sighed, "Aaaaah." Harley dropped his arms, put his face in his hands and let his body be wracked with sobs. Oh wait, wracked with laughter. Then everyone was laughing, applauding, banging their glasses on tables, and cheering.

Harley stood up and in his most polite manner announced, "I s'pose I gots to feed you now. Whatcha be having?"

My new friends had already discussed what their favorite dishes were and what they would try tonight. But I hadn't had a chance to even look at the menus.

"Harley I'm starving and need food. Let me take a look at a menu."

"No, no my sweet. Leave the feeding to ole Harley. You do the partakin' and 'preciatin' With a twinkle in his eye he finished, "Oh, and dump that mangy wild beast. I be your destiny!"

With that Harley look at the others, "It'd be my honor to feed y'all in gratitudes for bringin' my Janine to me."

"Sure Harley. Go for it." Gary said.

Harley bowed slightly as he back away from our table, "Welcome to the Big Easy." His free arm went flying upward again as everyone cheered and clapped.

"This isn't a restaurant," I said to the others, "this is a flash mob feeding frenzy."

"Ah, but there is more." Ryan assured me. Sure enough, as the evening progressed, we ate, we drank, and people brought out musical instruments. They played, we sang and many danced in the tight spaces between tables; all of us fully engaged in life.

The food. Oh my, the food. It just kept coming. We no sooner finished one dish and there was Harley with more Cajun cuisine for us to try. "This is Shut-My-Mouth-Clams. I tossed geoduck clams sum special dressin' of olive oil, lemon juice, sweet sweet chili, and fresh mint, been growed right back da kitchen door."

The group dug in and never said a word we were so busy savoring every morsel.

When Harley returned, we all smiled, Phyllis saying, "Well shut my mouth."

"You got it. So sumptuous you cain't speak. Now here be the main course," With that Harley placed a platter almost as big as our table, down for main feast. "Roasted ribs. Meatiest ribs yous ever be eatin'. My ribs be made with only a few 'gredients, my Cajun dry rub that my great granddaddy did hand down to the generations. Then it'd be a long, slow easy roast. Keeps 'em ribs moist and oh so tender."

Our mouths watered as the smells filled the air we breathed, ready for Harley to finish his explanation so they could dig in but first, "Here you be needin' these." Harley announced handing us bibs and extra napkins, "Eat...eat!" He exclaimed then booming joyous laughter rose from his chest.

I gobbled up one after the other. Juices and Cajun rub were all around my mouth, like a clown smile. Some of it made its way down to my bib. I didn't want to stop. Every bite of a rib craved another bite. Eating was something I did to be healthy, fit, to sustain life in the best way possible. This was a primordial experience, instinctive, life-giving and so darn delicious!

Finally sated, I turned to ask Phyllis the questions that had floated in and out of my mind all evening, "How can Harley pay for all of this, our meal? What will the owner say? I mean, he is the best waiter I have ever met and this place it's like family gathering or a block party, but?"

Phyllis jumped in, "Sure he's a great waiter, the best. Harley is even a better restaurateur."

"You mean...?"

"The Big Easy is Harley's place." Phyllis responded.

"Harley's?"

"Harley's." Phyllis looked at me for a moment, wondering if she should say more. "You don't know, do you?"

"Know what?" Now I was really confused. Harley, hulking, friendly but unassuming, protector of little dogs, was a restaurant owner, and a successful one if this evening was any indication. How did that happen? What more is there to his story?

"Harley has a story? No, I don't know it. Tell me."

Just then more rousing songs and cavorting overtook away any possibility of conversation. It was not obnoxious or disruptive, it was pure lively fun that everyone joined into as it ebbed and flowed like the wave at baseball games.

"Here's the short version." We stood by the front door as Phyliss spoke, "Harley's from New Orleans. Hurricane Katrina had shattered many lives. The waves came in six miles and were as high as thirty-five feet at times. Harley told us of seeing a sailboat caught about two-stories up in a cluster of trees. The devastation struck Harley and his mom who ran their family-owned restaurant that had been in existence for generations. Katrina swallowed it up. The massive waves swept away their livelihood, family traditions, and special recipes along with his mom."

Phyliss went on to tell me that Harley had stayed in the stadium shelter, too close to way too many people. One day he took his sleeping bag and knapsack to go look over the damage of his restaurant. He wanted to develop a plan to rebuild. After checking around, he learned that his mom was not in another shelter as he had hoped. She was one of the 1,400 people that died during the catastrophic category 3 hurricane.

The street where he had cooked countless meals and serve thousands of people, was in complete and utter ruin. A rubbish heap. He sat on a curb staring at the void around him, feeling the void inside of him. He drifted around, checking in on family that had survived, mostly going through the motions. A few months later, by the urging of a childhood friend who had started over in Washington, he left everything and everyone he had ever known and headed to Wenatchee determined to start over. Foremost, he wanted to honor his mom and all the family members that had dreamed of, then started and cultivated their family restaurant by sweat and perseverance. He heart was determined to start again.

Janine teared up. She looked at Harley then back at Phyliss who put her arm around her, "I know. Imagine what he went through to get to where he is today. Ya gotta love him."

With a big smile and hearty wave, Janine caught Harley's eye. "Hey Harley," she shouted over a few tables "You have yourself a great night. I'm heading out to buy a wedding dress!!"

They left to the boisterous cheers of Harley, all the diners singing as a guitarist plucked out, "Here Comes the Bride."

CHAPTER FIFTY-TWO

What is

THIS FEELING

I woke up and the world seemed different. In the stillness of the early morning, I laid quietly, trying to discern what was different in the world. Well, my world at any rate. Laying with one arm wrapped around Peaches and I felt... felt? Nope, the descriptive word eluded me.

The feeling was no longer numbness from all my sorrow and anger, the numbness that came when I shut down, afraid I would implode if I thought about what happened to Casey. This wasn't the lack of feeling, which is what I had been doing. It used to be that to feel was to ache in every part of my being. No, this was different; so very different. This was a good feeling.

Different, yes. Calmer? Yes, but not exactly.

I was petting Peaches, still asleep at my side as I basked in peacefulness, a sense of contentment. That was it. A feeling so alien I almost didn't recognize it. Happiness. Yes, that's it. I felt happy.

Then I felt scared, questioning myself. Do I have a right to feel happy? I like this feeling. But guilt seemed to hover around my mind. Millie was happy even with one leg. Harley is happy even with losing his mom and their restaurant. I want to be happy. Can I live with being happy? Yes. Yes, I can! I want to.

I thought about my new friends, especially Harley and all that he had been through. He chose a new life, he chose to be happy, laugh, celebrate and love. And oh, what a laugh. I ached to choose that too. Lifting Peaches above my prone body I announced, "I want to be happy." Peaches opened her sleepy eyes and looked down on my beaming face, then mewed in agreement. She's a bit of a bilingual show off.

Hey Peaches. Hey world. I am content. At peace. There are people feeding into my life in such a positive way. It's good to laugh and be a part of life again, like Harley and Millie and George.

Bringing Peaches onto my chest, I snuggled down into this awareness of being liberated; warm, alive, and curious. What does this mean? Where will this take me? Peaches stretched then gave me a good-morning kiss. I ruffled her fur declaring, "I'm happy Peaches. Happy!"

In acknowledgement Peaches bounced up, twirled around twice then bounded onto my chest. I sat up, rolling her onto the covers as I pushed down on the bed to create a bouncing motion tossing Peaches into the air. Peaches, not to be outdone, added her own energy to it. Before long we two girls were romping and rolling on the bed. Silly girls. Hopeful girls. Happy girls. A new day had begun.

I took my morning coffee out to my camp chair in the sun and sipped in the essence of being released from the heavy sorrow that had darkened my days. Without thinking, I extracted my phone from my pocket and dialed my mom.

My elusive mom, who rarely had cell coverage out in the middle of nowhere; my parents' favorite place to be when in their RV. Would there even be cell coverage? Yay, the phone rang.

"Janine?"

"Mom! Oh, mom, I didn't expect to reach you..."

All her motherly concerns poured out, "Is everything okay Jani? How are you? Where are you?"

I chuckled, "I'm fine mom, better than fine. Are you still in Yuma?"

"Oh good." My mom sighed with relief, "You sound, well you sound fine. No, we're in California. Slab City."

"Slab what, city? What is that! Where is that?"

"In the middle of nowhere." My mom said chuckling.

"I should have known!" I laughed, shaking my head. My mom, the late-blooming gypsy, "So where exactly is Slab City in California?"

"Look it up on Google, dear. It's just below Niland. It used to be a military base. When the military closed up and left, acres of desert remained with slabs of concrete where the installations used to be. People just started living out here. There's everything from broken down rusted old trailers and lean-to's right up to the most luxurious RV's."

"Only you and Dad could find a place like that." I said shaking my head at Peaches, who was perched on my lap, unleashed, outdoors. I am such a rebel!!

"Oh no, dear. There are hundreds of us here. There's even a little library, a church and a café that has jam sessions on Friday and Saturday nights. Oh, and a putting green. It's not grass. It's a mish mash of packed desert sand and artificial turf. That's where your dad is now, practicing his swing."

"Sounds like I need to look up this place. Hey, guess what mom? Today I'm headed out for a ride with some people I met yesterday. Work these dormant muscles of mine."

"That's great Janine. Though I would argue that you don't know about cranky muscles 'til you reach my age."

We chatted for a bit until I saw Phyliss walking my way. "Whoops I'd better get moving. It's almost time to ride. Love you mom and to dad too."

"Have a good ride. Be safe. Love you dear."

I called out to Phyliss, "Give me 5 minutes."

"Take your time. I'm just stretching my legs."

Ok, I have 5-minutes before the ride. I opened Google maps to check out where my parents were staying. I didn't hear footsteps but sensed someone nearby. It was Peaches that reacted with a low growl. Well, more like an asthmatic purr. Putting her paw on my phone got my attention.

As I looked at Peaches my peripheral vision caught a movement behind me. The Miller-tants, the camp hosts were standing ramrod straight scowling down at me.

"Oh, don't worry Peaches won't bite." I quipped.

Mrs. Miller-tant contorted her face and tilted her head slightly upward while her husband cleared his authoritative throat.

"We have no fear of your poor excuse for a dog. But it is evident that *you* have no fear of the rules. You did sign our Pet Control Form 367, section 5B, yet there sits your pet, unleashed!" I could see the thoughts crossing their wrinkled, scrunched up brows. This was going to be bad. I bet they double the fine. Would they go so far as to ask me to leave?

"Goooood morning all!" Boomed a familiar, drawling voice, "Great day ain' it? We coun't be askin' for a better day. Well, Mz. M. you sure be lookin' smart this fine mornin'. Did I tells y'all my plant finally gived me tomatoes? Ate one 'er them yeser'day. Mmmmmm, so sweet." He spoke his words in a way that made everyone's mouth water. "Here, let me get you a few for your noon meal." His big smile showed white teeth like a cheery hippo.

The two park hosts looked at each other, then looked at the offending camper, me. They seemed torn between a few nice ripe succulent tomatoes or taking action against a rule-breaker. It was a tough decision. I took the opportunity that this momentary distraction had created to snap the leash onto Peaches' collar.

"'There," Harley boomed, "See, dat mangy wild animal be'd secured. Com' on, you be soon tastin' my bes-ever tomatoes." More, big smile... more teeth. Ah my mountain-sized hero, here to stand between me and the two angry camp hosts about to extract a pound of my flesh. Go ahead,

Harley, bite their heads off with kindness! As they turned to follow Harley, I couldn't contain my smirk. Unfortunately, Mr. Miller saw it.

He turned back from following Harley, knowing he could not relinquish his responsibilities especially after being sneered at. "The next time, young lady..." He said sternly, "the fine will be doubled. Did you hear me? Doubled!" He abruptly turned and marched quickly off to catch up with Harley.

I peered down at my mangy wild animal, giggled and said, "Double trouble, that's you Peaches!"

Peaches responded with her kitten-like purr. *"Um, my growl."* she told me indignantly.

Casey has a crayon fisted in her hand as she makes
circles and lines on the paper I gave her. She changes
the color, gripping the crayon, for all she's worth,
moving back and forth across the paper.
"Be careful to stay on the paper, Casey."
"I am Mommy. I'm big now, I can write."
"How wonderful. What are you writing?"
"Don't you see my words, Mommy."
"I do peanut." Whoops, I may be caught
in my little white lie.
"Would you read it to me." Good comeback.
"Sure Mommy."
I sigh with relief.
Casey picked up the paper scribbled with about seven
different colors and reads affectionately,
"I love Mommy and Daddy and Peaches."

CHAPTER FIFTY-FOUR

I'm in Love

FELIX

Felix and Sofia were driving home, just about to turn onto their street. It had been a long day. One of the best they've had in quite some time. Who would have thought being around an ant hill of busy children would be so refreshing. And exhausting.

"I'm in love." Announced Felix.

"Well, you are glowing, but I thought it might be sweat." Sofia quipped.

"Did you see that no matter how many children piled into the backyard, I was still the center of attention." He beamed.

"Yes, you're Grampy. You're no longer Grumpy. Lydia, your loving six-year-old granddaughter kept running back to hug you and tell you the latest. My heart is soaring for you."

"Sofia, as much as I love you, have loved you all these years, Lydia stole my heart today."

"I can live with the competition." Sofia said as she squeezed Felix's hand.

Felix pulled into the driveway and as the garage door rose up, he looked at her, "Your wise words pushed me to move past all the walls I had built."

He inhaled deeply as a 100-watt smile lit up his face. "Mi amor. Oh, how I love you."

CHAPTER FIFTY-FIVE

I'm in Love

DANNY

D o I call my sister Janine. "Hi this is your little bro Danny...um I'm in love."

I don't know who to tell. It's not like it's a big secret. Everyone around me, us, can see it. But can they feel it like I feel it, like this deep pulsing sonar that fans out powerfully moving me in the direction of Melissa. When I first came to pastor this church there she was, a kind, willing volunteer. She caught my heart that first day becoming much more to me with each interaction. his stumbled into dating.

Instead, I picked up my phone to call Melissa as I finished tiding up the kitchen after my dinner. Her image was always right before my eyes; willowy, goofy, bouncy yet determined and always ready to help. It amazed me that she remembered everyone's name, even someone she'd only met once. It endeared people to her as she greeted them by their name with her cheerful smile. I struggled with names, which as a priest was not one of my better talents.

"Hey Melissa, I found a new hike for us on Friday. It's best to leave early." I said holding my cell to my ear as I rinsed off my dinner dish.

"Define early Danny. You know I'm the night owl of us birds."

"Will 7:30 work?"

Melissa groaned suggesting, "If we leave at 9:00 I can make us lunch to take along. And no Danny, not protein bars. A real lunch. Plus, I can drink my coffee as I slave over our meal."

"An honest to God, solid, delectable real lunch?? Yup 9 o'clock works for me. I should warn you; part of the trail has multiple switchbacks. It can be an arduous climb through tall pines and fern undergrowth. The best part is when we arrive at this sunlit shimmering emerald pond. I have a favorite log where I always sit, um to eat my protein bar."

Melissa responded with confidence, "All these hikes you've taken me on was to build me into a true hiker. I knew it. And, Danny, I can do it!!"

"Great. I'll pick you up, bright and early. I mean at 9:00."

My mind drifted through the evening as I thought about Melissa and tomorrow.

Tomorrow. At that lake. On that log. Eating the lunch she will prepare. I want Melissa to know how I feel. I'm in love. I want to tell her in that most perfect setting.

Grabbing his cell phone from the counter, he punched in Ken's number as he thought, I ought to have Ken on speed dial.

"Danny? An evening call. This has to be good."

Danny jabbered on for a world record probably giving Ken a wrestler's cauliflower ear as he "ah ha", "yup" "sure I get it". Danny peppered him with questions about love, how do you know it's real, lasting? In between the questions he enumerated, in finite detail, all the ways and reasons he loved Melissa.

"Well Danny this is wonderful. Having someone to love is the best. I love Janine."

"Oh, sorry man, I didn't mean to stir up all the hurt."

"No, no. You have to understand I've loved Janine since we were kids. I loved her when we dated, married, when we had Casey. My love for her remains no matter what. I will always love her. There will never be another woman for me. I don't need to have her loving me back, though that would be nice. My love for her is the foundation of my being. It is and will be with me to my dying day. It is a comfort and a contentment even with its sorrow. I'm good Danny. But you, man, you're airborne, out in the stratosphere. When you come back to earth or after the hike, let me know how it went."

"Sure bro. I don't think I can sleep."

"I expect not. But I can, bye Danny. Thanks for the call. It made my evening."

Preparing for bed, Ken stepped out of the shower, grabbed a towel and began to dry off. Over the hum of the fan, he heard his cell phone ringing. Two calls in one night, who could it be this time?

Caller ID, Danny.

"Love Story part two?"

"Hey Ken. I forgot to tell you. Janine will be at Dungeness in a few days. She texted me tonight after a ride with some new friends she made."

"New friends. Riding. That's fantastic. This week is the annual art festival in Langley." He said trying to figure out how he could get to Dungeness, knowing Danny would advise against it. This was the week where artists and vendors from across Washington and beyond came to celebrate, sell, and talk art. It was a major event. A time when the shop thrived. They could barely keep product on the shelves.

"Oh right. With your dad out sailing in parts unknown, you'll be going morning to night. Well, at any rate, I can keep you posted." Danny honestly thought it was for the best that Ken had something to keep him tied to Langley and stop him from going to Dungeness. He felt Janine wasn't ready for that reunion just yet.

"Thanks, Danny. Yes, please let me know. You're a lifeline."

Chapter Fifty-Six

I'm in Love

Janine

I Janine, no longer married, no longer a mother. So this wasn't a planned thing. It morphed into being alive, taking a part in life. In the evenings, the bike crew and I hung out at Harley's The Big Easy. It never took long for people to unsnap cases, bring out various instruments and begin jamming. Sometimes a voice of beautiful clarity flitted across us from somewhere beyond where we could see. Romantic. Yes, and earthy, organic, natural.

In the morning, we gathered at Phyllis's campsite drinking coffee or tea while the guys grilled up breakfast. Ryan was always extra attentive towards me. He would tease, joke and even wink at me. Wink. He made me feel seen, attractive. Sometimes Harley joined us when he closed the restaurant early, got to bed at a decent hour and was awake when we were up. That was always a treat.

As we ate, we'd review our plans for that day's ride, usually 50-60 miles. Peaches would be with me soaking up all the love and petting she got as she moved from lap to lap, displaying her sweetest face, awaiting a piece of bacon. Her leash dangled from her collar in accordance with the rules. Harley may not always be around to save me from the delightful [tongue-in-cheek] Miller-tants and their multitude of fines they were eager to pounce on someone.

I'd bring her back to the van, finish packing for the ride and meet up everyone as we headed out. Even living under the thumb of our militant hosts, the days slipped by easily. My most notable delight, was that I started to feel. My soul breathed in the vistas as we rode, the smells awakened my appreciation as they radiated up from the diverse terrain. I even flirted a bit with Ryan riding next to me.

We kept up an 18-mph pace. The riders naturally created a loosely formed pace-line to have a few moments of reducing the pedaling effort resulting from the draft off the rider in front of them. It was a satisfying experience riding with accomplished cyclists. The sun, the laughter, teasing, alternating the lead and who was drafting, all penetrated and stirred up a hunger, a distant memory starved for too long. I craved life and was feasting on each morsel. Ryan? His wink and caring attentiveness?

The word finally came to me. Love.

I was in love. In love with life, the exhilaration of sharing rides, the newness of everything around me. Yet more than that.

Phyllis hoped it was Ryan, her brother who was putting such a big smile on my face. Merriment spilling out from his eyes like fireflies twinkling away on warm summer nights.

I guess it could have been Ryan. Hoped it was Ryan. It wasn't. It went back further than that. I missed and loved my home, the town I grew up in, Langley.

When that realization came, I knew it was time to continue on with my quest to Dungeness. I explained to my new friends the time had come to head northwest. I left a few days later, after saying farewell during morning coffee. I was thankful Harley was there as well.

Propelled from inside my heart to embrace what was ahead. With all that had happened, it felt like ages ago since I left Arizona. My final destination less than a day away.

Lots of hugs, good cheer and me repeating multiple times, "Hey, really keep in touch. Riding with all of you has been the best."

Phyllis hugged me whispering, "Not Ryan huh?'

"Sorry. He's great but…"

"No, no. Not a problem Janine. I get it. We definitely will ride together, again."

More hugs and well wishes surrounded me as Peaches and I got in the van and drove off. Before pulling onto the highway, I text my parents and Danny like I had done regularly, to give them headlines of my day. Then I was on my way.

I'm in love. Who? What? Home?

Fill in the blank. So far, I can't. But love permeates my every cell.

CHAPTER FIFTY-SEVEN

I'm in Love

BRIAN

For Janine's parents, Brian and Pam, it had become their habit to pray before the next leg of their trip. They would unhook the rig and battening down anything that moves. Pam double check each the drawers and the fridge, listening for the click that assured it was locked in place. Once, the fridge door flew opened when Brian took a rather sharp turn. Perishables spilling out everywhere as a puddle of milk spread across the tile. Lesson learned.

They turned in their seats partially facing each other holding hands across the wide gap between them, bowed their heads and prayed. Their evening prayers always included thankfulness, the kids, family and those they knew of who were struggling. Traveling prayers were as the Lord led and for safety as they drove.

"Amen." Brian finished. As he was releasing Pam's hands, she held on tighter.

"Brian, I feel it's time to go home."

With the hum of the engine, they remained still, not speaking just holding hands, drawing on their own thoughts and feelings.

"Pam, yes, I agree, it's time. Is this about Janine?"

"It is and it isn't. I want to be there for our daughter."

"So go directly home to Langley or to Dungeness?"

"We can travel at a comfortable pace. I still want to spend a a day or two in Glacier National Park. I think Dungeness is for Janine. I want to honor that. One day she'll be ready to see us and I want to be within arm's reach to hold her again."

Brain tensed. Pam recognized his anger. She had addressed it several times as gently as possible. Pam understood that Brian typically pushed down emotions and kept going, rarely seeing that it seeped out as anger. Sure, there were indications of this when they were raising the kids and building careers. Brian had been to many conferences and workshops which included anger management. He had put that knowledge to good use, which had benefited their home life. But that intensity that came out as anger was and would probably always be the thorn in Brian's side.

When their granddaughter Casey died, Brian's emotional self control became as fragile as gossamer threads, When used to create a delicate scarf is was exquisite. Yet with a slip of the hand it could be ripped apart. Brian's sweet love was like gossamer, but when being ripped apart he quickly wrapped in the protective armor of anger. Hot anger at times.

"Brian. You're tensing up. What just stirred up inside you? Honey, share it with me, you know that always helps."

He turned off the engine wanting to talk but barely able to hold back his emotions. Like molten lava the heat of his feelings rose up and poured forth. Pam mostly listened but also tried to clarify what he said. After venting, Brian was able to more calmly articulate what losing Casey and Janine was like for him.

The intensity of his word pierced her at times, but as Brian became more composed a reality played out before them. Acknowledging the truth, speaking the pain that he tended to keep crammed down, seemed to help.

Right before her eyes, Brian demeanor changed. Venting, then speaking his hurt out loud was transformative.

Pam silently thanked God for his mercies that are new every morning.

With a loving squeeze of Pam's hand he let go, restarted the engine, put the big rig in drive and they headed out.

"I love you Pam and I know it hasn't been easy for you these past months as I relearn how to deal with all my feelings. Feelings are for women." He smiled. "I don't know how you do it. There are too many thoughts that are swirling around at any given time in my mind. Each has a feeling attached. I know how to stuff them down and push them away. I can see that method really doesn't solve anything. This really helped. Thanks for letting me spew."

Pam nodded, her expression was of agreement and compassion seeing Brian struggling to get it right.

Brain said over the rumble of the rig coming to life. "You keep me centered, focused on what is healthy and good."

"We've never dealt with something as substantial as this before. Today was a good start for you. Can I ask you to lean on me, vent when you need to, before things build up inside of you?"

"Yes, I can do that. I do love you so, Pam."

"I love you, Brian."

CHAPTER FIFTY-EIGHT

Dungeness

SPIT

I decided to go through Oak Harbor to Coupeville and catch the ferry over to the Olympic Peninsula. I wasn't avoiding taking the Mukilteo to Clinton ferry, which would take me within miles of my hometown of Langley. Langley was not my destination, Dungeness was. A destination I was ready to reach without distraction.

My plan was to stop the night before at Deception Pass State Park. That would allow me time to be rested before the final trek. Or to chicken out if I needed to. I didn't need to. That stop became pure enjoyment. You can't beat Deception Pass for scenery with the expansive bridge, the twisted trees and secluded beach. All that would have soothed any jittery nerves but I was already calm and actually, expectant.

Or was I shut down. Closed off again. Unwilling to feel.

Strangely it was the exact opposite. The *"I'm in love"* state of mind and heart was awakened further by the aromatic scents unique to the Pacific Northwest.

It was like I was floating in a meadow of wildflowers, clothed in a flowing dress as I rose up to dance under the afternoon sun. It warmed me, bringing a flush to my cheeks. Love.

There is no fear in love, but perfect love casts out fear. Yes, I remember now, that's a verse from 1 John. That's how I felt.

I missed the ferry. Dang. I had headed out in a timely manner, but there she sailed halfway to the peninsula. Reading the schedule I saw that the crossing times had changed for the season. I parked my car in line and got out with Peaches to walk around and stretch my legs knowing I had plenty of time before the next ferry.

"Finally, girl. I do need to use the facilities you know."

"Yes Peaches, and there are some lovely places for you to squat." I led her toward a Fort Casey State Park trail as she sniffed her heart away, her nose wiggling like a Jello square.

We returned to the Keystone Ferry landing in plenty of time to watch the ferry coming in from across the way. It was about fifteen-minutes out. While sitting on a bench enjoying the view of the Olympic Mountains, a sea monster steadily emerged from the water in front of me. I jumped. Peaches squealed. A dark ominous oversized round-headed creature with seaweed draped across its skull continued up out of the darkened depths.

Oh. Okay.

Well. Not a monster.

Sorry.

It was a scuba diver in a wet suit.

Peaches wasn't so sure it was human, as she tucked in under my arm.

A nearby sign reminded me the area was called Fort Casey Underwater Park, one of the best for scuba diving. I had heard there is even octopi in the waters. You would think growing up on Whidbey that Ken and I would have given this a try. Unless we swam, in a pool doing laps, our sports tended to be on dry land and I was still fine with that.

We were back in the car when ferry arrived and a river of cars flowed off. Then it was time for us to drive onboard. Workers in bright yellow vests waved me toward a lane. At the head of that lane, another yellow-vester urged me forward with her hands beckoning me forward. Once parked, drivers and passengers did not have to remain in their cars. Peaches and I preferred to go up onto the inside deck and look out the windows. If it was sunny we'd go out on the open deck and feel the wind in our hair. One time the mighty wind was wickedly strong and almost blew us overboard. With hair blowing all over and me huddling Peaches close to my chest, trying to get back inside, we weren't quite as picturesque as the Titanic scene.

The ferry docked and disembarked in Port Townsend then headed back toward Sequim. Ok, more trivia if you ever need to know this. Sequim is called the blue hole. The reason...ta da: Western Washington has plenty of rain. At the northern end of the peninsula Sequim usually can count on sunshine and blue skies at some point during every day. This is because of protection from the rain shadow caused by the Olympic Mountains. Seattle equals rain. Sequim equals the blue hole. Now you know. PS: That's why our family got into the routine of camping at Dungeness. More blue skies, less rain. A real plus for campers.

To get to Dungeness, the road winds out from Sequim for quite a while. Like a harmless garter snake traveling around, catching a few rays. A driver could almost feel like they've missed a turn or got lost. It's the feeling I get almost every time I do this drive. I tend to look around, not sure of were I am. Am I even in Washington. The whiffs of salty water, towering red cedar, hemlock and luxurious rich soil reassured me. I was close to Dungeness. I took it all in through my nose, as my eyes tried to take in the scenery. My skin tingled as the ocean air caressed my arms. Peaches' ears perked up and her nose started to wiggle as she turned in circles. She leaned onto the arm rest to look out the window. She knew. Her tiny nose remembered. Her whole body remembered.

The Strait of Juan de Fuca was calling. Victoria BC just across the strait would glitter at night fall, reflecting on the water. As I pulled into the campground, I was delighted to see a large madrona tree with its red peeling bark stretching its curvy branches far and wide. This tree had welcomed me, us, for years and years. I've watched it grow up. It felt like family, like coming home.

Abruptly, I slammed on my brake, jolting Peaches from her perch. Sorry baby.

I didn't want to be home; to enter through the check-in station and try to recall which camp site I liked the best. This was a bad idea. A very bad idea. The smell that I cherished a moment ago, made me gag. I couldn't look at the red cedars beckoning me to enter. My arms felt chilled.

What was I thinking. I was not ready. Not yet. No. Definitely. Not. Ready.

I pulled off the side of the road opposite the madrone tree that was reaching out to grab me in its clutches.

Gripped in fear I managed to dial Danny. "Janine. Janine?"

Silence. A gasp.

"Janine, talk to me. Where are you? What's wrong."

I heard Danny's voice quietly praying. I couldn't discern the words, but the cadence was encouraging.

"Danny." I whispered, "I'm at the spit. I can't go in. I just can't. I'm scared."

He was still praying but I knew he was listening. Then I heard him end with, "Perfect love casts out fear Father. Jesus, we need you. Amen."

Softly, "Janine. You are ready for this." With gentle reassurance he said, "I'll go with you."

I pulled the van further off the drive and shut it off to wait, "How long will it take for you to get here?"

"I'll go with you on your cell. Come on. Together. Ready?"

"Yes. No." I whimpered reluctantly turning the van's engine back on. I place my phone securely in the dash holder on speaker.

"Have you come to the madrona tree yet?"

I swallowed, "I'm across from it. It's trying to kill me. It looks evil."

"How can 'Annie' be evil?"

Stunned, I replied, "Oh my gosh. Annie! How did you remember that name?"

"You named the tree Annie because of all the red wavey branches that look like hair to you. What were you, eight or nine? I never got it but, when I said so, you went full bore on me. You could get quite bossy you know. You drummed that name into me. Every time we were near the tree you looked at me sternly and asked, *What's her name?* How could I ever forget that tree. Furthermore, my insistent sister, wavy-haired Annie is not evil. Let me hear you say it."

My little brother had reversed the roles, taking charge. Dutifully, I repeated, "Annie is not evil." I was almost convinced. Not.

"Now, please take a deep breath, put the van in drive and let's get moving. I love you. I'm right here with you."

How did Danny take charge and not sound bossy. That's probably what made him a good priest.

I did what he asked me to do. To ease my nerves, I narrated as I drove.

"I'm coming up on the main gate and the equestrian trail. I made it through the gate."

"Good. Good. Anyone at the dump station."

I had to laugh. We always said that same statement ever since our parents taught us how to dump. Our first few times we didn't connect the black water hose [poo-hose] correctly. After a few smelly, messy mistakes, we never forgot to wear gloves and secure the connection. From then on, we giggled and laughed as we checked out the other dumpers. Are they connected properly? Do they have gloves on? Are they making a mess like we once did?

"No people dumping." I reported.

I told Danny I was about to turn into Loop 1. We always stayed in any of the sites between 12 and 16. He suggested I try something different, Loop 2 and look for a site around #40. I did.

"Hey, there are 'hiker-biker' campsites here."

I heard him smile. "Just right for a biking chic I know."

"I'm backing in. Hold on."

He must have heard me put the van in park. "Now, sis, I recommend you set up just as you did at each stop on your way up. Explore the area, just chill, read, whatever. No need to push yourself. You'll know when you're ready."

"I'll call you. You can come with me."

"Call me after. This is a meaningful time between you and the Lord. He will be with you."

"Danny, I haven't prayed much or done anything God-wise for.... well, I don't even remember when."

"Oh Janine, God loves you. He has never left you or forgotten you. He has walked with you through every one of those horrible days. He was the down-comforter you kept wrapped around you as you hid in Aunt Sally's guest room. He was the blooming Argentine cactus that greeted you the first day you ventured out. He was Aunt Sally bringing you a tray of breakfast knowing you wouldn't eat but a bite. He gave mom and dad the courage to keep coming to Aunt Sally's trying to reach you. Even after all the times they ended up sitting in the hall by your closed door when you refused to see them. They prayed healing over you, lifting you up to God. Best of all, He was the one that got you lost when you took a drive and came upon the van you are now sitting in. God has always been there, and he is there with you now."

I sat stunned, absorbing Danny's words.

Finally, I mouthed. "Amen."

"Talk with you later, sis."

"Thanks Danny. You're a good traveling companion."

Although there were utility connections for the van, I didn't even bother to set up. I made a cup of chamomile tea for its calming effect and sat down on the bed. Thankfully, Peaches made room for me. I placed the tea on the little shelf/table to the side and took out my journal. After sipping my tea, writing and thinking about "the God who's with me" I took Peaches for a short walk. Back in the van, we both dozed off.

CHAPTER FIFTY-NINE

A Vision

You know that disoriented feeling you get sometimes when you first wake up. That's how I came out of my nap. Warmth radiated across my chest, soothing, relaxing, like I was swaddled in a robe after a bath. Oh, wait, it was Peaches sleeping on top of me. That was a new one. Not wanting to disturb her I just laid there, plus I had to come out of that fugue state.

"Ok, Dungeness am I ready?" In my mind I bounced between determination and trepidation. The more I woke up, the more I didn't feel hesitant. No, it was more than a feeling.

I was seeing something. Almost like a dream, but not. Like an IMAX theater submerged in images. Casey. It was my cherished daughter, Casey. The image became more clear. She wasn't alone, though I couldn't make out all the people around her. Without totally recognizing the person right next to her holding her hand, I knew from within, it was Jesus.

Casey and Jesus. Casey is okay. Casey is surrounded by perfect love. Her smile was beaming as if she was the sunrise itself.

I cried.

Joy. Pure joy.

Casey and Jesus.

She let go of His hand and started to run, laugh, then she was skipping. My always-active sweet little Casey, playing joyfully with Jesus smiling as she did so.

CHAPTER SIXTY

Walking Along

A FAMILIAR PATH

My heart felt light at having seen Casey. The early evening whispered night's soft arrival. I wanted to walk, to be out in the freshness of nature, to get out of the van and stretch my legs. With all of me, my body, mind and soul, I yearned to embrace all that I loved about Dungeness.

Peaches and I meandered around. I was smiling thinking of Casey. Peaches was marking every bush and barking at squirrels as she pulled on the leash.

"Ah Peaches, you are not a boy, you do not mark your territory. And did you notice those squirrels are bigger than you."

"Hey mom, do you want dinner or what? Girls can hunt too, you know. I am fearless."

The wide-open expanse closed into a long pathway through trees, the branches reaching across to hold hands, producing a tunnel. The filtered light encouraged me onward surrounded by the piney arms of nature. We came to the bluff trail and started walking upward, pausing often to take in the captivating view. The water below pounding the rocky cliffs that held the sea in check. The view, the sounds, revived my soul. The cliffs gave way to a long section of beach where activity ebbed and flowed throughout the day and into the evening.

When I could see the uppermost point of the path, I noticed a new bench. Perfect. I had always believed there needed to be a bench at the apex. Probably every time Ken, Casey and I took this walk I would remark, "They ought to put a bench here. There isn't a better view around."

"Are you giving me another wood crafting project." He would respond.

"Ooooh, I never thought of that." I'd say while batting my eyes at him.

"Daddy, I want a bench. You can make it. I know you can. You can make anything."

After having taken the later ferry, the long drive to Dungeness, then falling asleep, the sun was contemplating taking its leave. Dusk was close. I wanted to get to the new bench to sit for a while before heading back. I hustled Peaches along.

"No more hunting and marking little girl, we have a destination."

The bench faced north with trees to the west shading it as the sun was going down. I looked beyond the trees and saw an artist's work. God was painting the sky as only he can. Oranges softly flowing into pinks with bold slashes of burgundy adding drama. It made me catch my breath. There were enough clouds for the colors to be magnified as they stretched and blended. In awe, I sat down on the bench holding Peaches and watched as God's extraordinary handiwork played out majestically before my eyes.

Peaches wiggled to get down. Still on her leash, I gave her some length to explore as I took a better look at where I was sitting. It wasn't just your basic wood or concrete bench. It was made with a great deal of skillfulness and attention to detail. I glided my hand over the arms, the seat. Smooth. Thoroughly sanded and finished. It looked like teak. Good, it will last for years.

The originality was stunning. On the underside of the arms were twisted branches that went back and around on itself. Turning toward the back of the bench, I saw sand-dollars etched into the wood. That made me think of our times at Neah Bay, the furthest northwest point of the peninsula. We could pick up as many sand dollars as we could carry. One year we helped Casey, and a few other four-year-old friends paint them to make Christmas ornaments. Turning further, I saw a dedication plaque. Of course, that made sense. Something this beautiful was made from love. I read the sandblasted inscription.

In Loving Memory of
Casey Dunleavy
2010 – 2016
"Jesus Loves Me This I Know."

I had run out of tissues. I let the final vestiges of pain, sorrow and isolation pour out of my eyes. Hiccup sobs and gasps. A moment of composure led to another bout as deep-rooted wounds in my heart found release.

Slowly Jesus breathed life into the my soul. His love refilled the void left by all that had poured out. His arms of comfort wrapped around what had been shattered, holding my broken pieces together. Who else but Jesus could flood my soul with love. comfort and peace?

He turned my sadness into joy. Not that "I'm happy, happy, happy," joy. He bestowed on me the joy of knowing, without a doubt, that Casey was in the best place any one of us would hope to be. Jesus loved Casey. He would love her every day for eternity. Jesus would love me here, until I saw him face to face with Casey by his side.

In that moment I knew I could go on. I could have a life. My baby was safe and cherished. So was I, with an everlasting love.

CHAPTER SIXTY-ONE

Beyond

WHAT WE CAN IMAGINE

The distant lights of Victoria BC, across the strait, started to glow as the setting sun said good night. It was getting quite dark. Groups of people were below on the beach with campfires; singing, laughing, playing and cheering each other on. I wondered what game they were playing.

As I checked my phone, hoping it had enough battery life left for the flashlight to guide me home, Peaches barked. I looked at her. She was dancing and pulling on her leash. She wasn't alarmed so neither was I. I looked to my right, where she was trying to go. She was doing her twirling-welcome routine, ready to greet someone and get petted. Which meant all was good. Someone was on the path heading toward us.

About fifteen feet away a man slowed then stood quietly. He seemed a bit apprehensive. I thought, that was courteous of him. My eyes adjusted to the dark and focused better. I knew that shape.

Ken.

CHAPTER SIXTY-TWO

Always

AND FOREVER

The air between them stopped, as did Janine's heart. After months of isolation, she could not grasp the reality of the person standing before her. Janine held her breath, closed her eyes then slowly opened them.

Ken.

He moved closer, putting his back against the rail, one foot resting on the lower rung, his hands in his pockets. Janine stood up and leaned sideways on the fence facing Ken. Not too close but able to see his expression. As a distraction, she turned her head to watch people settling in around a campfire on the beach below the bluff.

He softly cleared his throat. His own personal yearnings pushed against his chest frantic for release. Holding himself in check, he searched for the right words.

"Janine." Was all he could say.

She turned to face him. "Ken. Yours?" She nodded toward the bench.

"Yes, mine."

"It's beyond beautiful. Your best work yet."

They both stood silently.

Ken started again, "Has this trip been good for you?"

"The bench is stunning, impressive. There are no words. And yes, Ken the trip has been good in some very unexpected ways." She hesitantly brushed his arm. "I am forever sorry for how I left, so abruptly. How I hurt you on top of us losing Casey. I truly was not in my right mind. The mind where we were always together.... where we built a life together, supported each other."

"There is nothing you could ever do that would make me not love you."

"Oh Ken. I do love you; I do. In spite of what I've done."

More silence ensued as Janine absorbed Ken's words.

"Do you want to try again?" he asked softly.

It was only the quick blink of Janine's eyes that gave any hint that she heard him. She stood stone still. Stiff. Finally, she shook her head back and forth. No.

"Oh Ken." She sighed. "You mean like a story book ending. Where we live happily ever after?" Her words flat, heavy-laden from too much reality.

"No Janine. We had storybook already. We lost it in the most horrible way."

"Then what?"

"I don't know. It's like the people who come into the shop. They see the wooden trains and fall in love with them. Some buy them, bring them home and place them on a shelf. They polish them, take care of them and view them in all their perfection. Then you've got the guy and his son. They can barely choose which they like best, they love them all. They make their purchase and head on home, to play with their trains. And play...and play. The trains get beat up, pieces are broken off, the sheen is dulled in some areas, but dad and son share a love for those trains. Those times build memories which, in turn, build their history."

"Are you calling us a train wreck?"

"Well, we sure had the picture-perfect life, like those trains on a shelf. We've also had a train wreck. We've been roughed up and parts have been broken. Janine, I think the love is still there, for both of us. This is part of our history." Ken reached for her hand and she let him take it. "We're tarnished. We lost all our innocence, Janine. I know that. We don't have to lose each other."

"It's so hard Ken. Maybe too hard."

"Maybe it's easier when you do it side by side." He paused, reached for her other hand and turned toward her. "You love me, right Janine?"

"Always Ken. Always." The love she had felt but could not identify. rose up. Ken. She loved Ken.

Ken moved his left hand into his pocket and took out a small gift box. He fumbled with it then held out it to Janine. "Will you marry me?'

She knew the box held a ring, but hesitantly opened it. What she saw baffled her. What was going on; was this really happening? How could this be her wedding ring. The wedding ring she had ripped off her finger and thrown into the woods.

"Oh Ken..." Was all she could say as tears welled up in her eyes and her voice got hoarse.

After a moment she asked, "How? It's my wedding ring that, in a fit of hysteria, I threw into the woods." Something Janine had since regretted. A moment she could never get back. Well, almost never.

Ken's crooked smile. "Your dad saw you throw it, with that pitcher's arm of yours. He scoured the area for days until he found it."

"My dad, really. Can we do this, Ken?"

"Janine, we can't *not* do this. We have to do this. For our sake, for Casey's sake, in memory of Casey, we should live. And love."

Janine looked toward the beach and saw several firepits glowing brightly. No, it wasn't a storybook ending, but she had come here to start over, to find her life. Why not find it with the man she loved.

Afraid of the power of her own emotions, she took a step back, "Yes Ken, let's do this together."

"Oh Janine, you are my heart. I love you."

After a few moments he spoke softly, "Um, confession time."

Janine braced for it. Did he date someone? Was there entanglements? Maybe he sold their house?

He admitted, "Technically you are still my wife. I never finalized the divorce by signing the papers."

He put out his hand for the gift box, removed the ring and placed it on her hand. "Where it belongs."

She couldn't hold back any longer and fell into his arms. "You are where I belong. Oh, how I have missed you."

Around the fire on the beach below, cheers rose up followed with whoops and hollers. It was as if all those campers were cheering for them.

Janine and Ken's hearts were doing the same.

Peaches was swirling and wiggling and yipping. *"My daddy-Ken is back, My daddy-Ken. Yay."*

Chapter Sixty-Three

As Time

Went On

Over a year after I had turned to see Ken standing on the bluff at Dungeness, we had been back to the campground once already and were planning to go there again in a few months. We were also considering finding a different destination. I championed the Oregon coast. Peaches was on my side.

That night, a year ago, at Dungeness with Peaches snuggled in between us, Ken and I talked into the early hours. We were both tentative at first until he took my hands, again and finally my wall of shame tumbled down. I was overwhelmed with a desire to hold him closer and... well you get the picture.

Instead, we talked about our grieving and how different it was for each of us. I told him about getting lost and finding the camper van as he laughed at me, reminding me that my superpower was taking wrong turns. Speaking of camping he asked if I knew my parents were headed back to Whidbey, were probably arriving there soon.

"I put them through the ringer. How did they ever manage?"

Peaches was displaced as Ken tightened his arms around me. "They used to force themselves to try to be somewhat cheerful when we spoke. It was awkward but we all wanted to stay connected. This last time they sounded hopeful and looking forward to being home for when you were ready to visit them."

I sighed with relief. Ken kept his hold on me.

He shared his desire to build something in Casey's honor as a remembrance; he talked his plan over with Danny, how Felix got in touch with him and how he and his wife Sofia asked if they could make the sandblasted plague. "We worked together to come up with the inscription."

"Felix and Sofia. The people with the trailer? In the back of my mind, I wondered what happened to them and what a burden they carried. That plaque. I heard Casey singing when I read it!"

"I was zoned in on working with the wood, getting the right wording, arranging for permits. You know all the details. It wasn't until Felix and Sofia secured a place for the bench at Dungeness that it hit me. I heard Casey singing too. We all shed some tears that day. Oh, and get this, they actually live in Sequim where Felix is a part-time pastor." Ken proceeded to tell me about how God had broken through Felix's guilt and how he came to feel worthy to celebrate his 6-year-old granddaughter's birthday and openly love her."

He went on, "I used to have no doubt about my faith and the prompting of the Holy Spirit in my life."

Janine recalled, "I know how you had an ongoing conversation throughout the day with God, as you worked, sanded a piece of wood or helped a customer."

Continuing Ken said, "When we lost Casey, when she went to spend eternity with Jesus, that all changed."

"I used to feel that too when I prayed, close to God." Janine said, "At times there is this infinite longing for Casey and I'd want to cry into his arms. But most of the time, God seems so far away."

Nodding, Ken agrees, "Life seems to be a constant ebbing and flowing, sometimes churning, even drowning. I think of Casey every day. The sorrow of it comes in waves. Sometimes it pounds the breath out of me and it feels like I will never breathe again." Ken gasps just thinking about it. They talked into the early hours details no one else knew or felt like they did as Casey's parents.

Interspersed with the many words, they would be entwined in each other's arms, laying quietly for a long periods of time just breathing. Sighing. Connected.

CHAPTER SIXTY-FOUR

While

WE WERE APART

I started telling Ken about my adventures and what I had learned along the way. "I met camp hosts Millie and George, the best people ever." On I went about their lives as we laughed, then nestled closer. Ken agreed, "Hmm, I agree with Millie. We all do have our sorrows."

I could not leave out the other camp hosts, the Miller-tants or my biking buddies. Ken ribbed me saying he thought I could use a little structure and that we ought to visit the Miller-tants in the future for further training on following rules.

Ken told me, "I've been biking a lot around Whidbey, but I am needed more and more at the shop. Dad is off sailing. Mom flies to places where dad is when he will be docked for more than a day. They explore, try new foods, and go to museums to get a sense of the local history. His sailing buddy's wife joins them sometimes as well. Mom refuses to be on the boat when dad unties it from the dock. She just waves her airline ticket from solid ground and calls a ride-share."

"Ah Ken. Isn't that sweet. Wait. Speaking of your dad, isn't this the big art festival week at Langley?" He nodded yes as I continued, "I mean don't you need to be there. You DO need to be there. Especially with your dad being gone."

He pulled me firmly into his muscular chest; his body generated warmth like a fireplace on a cold night. He breathed, "There is no place I have to be but with you. Ever."

Ken remained the perfect gentleman even sleeping on a backpacking mattress in the bed of his truck. Though, he was more than willing to share my coffee in the morning. Our conversation naturally moved from what we had gone through to where we were going. We agreed that wherever it was, we were going together.

"And me too. I'm going too." Peaches let us know. We both petted her with reassurance.

Our first destination was home, Whidbey. Langley. It was a touch difficult since we had two vehicles. We had to drive back separately. No hand holding, touch, being near to each other. Clever as always, Ken called me. We put our phones on speaker and drove together.

"Did you know Danny's in love?"

"No" I squealed trying to watch the road. "In love? Well, that is something. My little brother in love."

"Silly in love."

"Tell me everything."

When we were on the ferry, we made a few important calls to our families. "We're coming home and we're coming home together." You can imagine everyone's reactions. The best call was to my swooning little brother, Danny-in-love. What a joy to listen to him gush about Melissa.

CHAPTER SIXTY-FIVE

Island

LIFE

I didn't work for the first few months. I found I needed to acclimate myself to everyday life. I helped Ken at the store a few days a week just to be around him. We had dinner and played games with my parents a few times a week. Ken's mom often joined us. I even cooked for some of those gatherings.

Oh, that's something that changed in me. I craved being around my family. It was a joy rather than having to remind myself to make room for them as I did in my previous busy life. I didn't want to ever be that busy again or always striving for the future. Today, the here and now, every moment was what mattered to me. We both knew how quickly life could change. Thankfully, that meshed well with Ken's personality, who had always been Mr. Homebody.

Along the way we renewed our vows. We were going to keep it, "just family" until I was chatting with Phyllis who felt like family. I mean she had visited a while back, even biking Whidbey with Ken and I. True to being Phyllis, she invited herself.

"Oh, you want to come?" I replied.

"Absolutely. Even if it's not vows with my brother Ryan." She teased.

"It's going to be simple, nothing all out. You know, my parents' backyard simple."

"Fine with me. I can do simple." Phyliss responded.

She lied.

On our renewal day, I was at our house with my mom fussing over me. Tucking this, brushing down that, oohing and aahing as she placed flowers in my hair. Still the hippy. Ken had gone on ahead. You know, so he wouldn't see me. I mean, he always sees me in jeans and t-shirts. I wanted to milk this for all it was worth. A dress. Fancy at that. With a mani-pedi and my hair tamed. Well somewhat.

As we approached my parent's house, I could hear the family laughing and talking in the backyard. I was excited that Danny and Melissa were here for a week. Danny was doing the ceremony. Plus, I would have plenty of time to get to know Melissa better.

The word must have spread that mom and I had arrived. There was a sudden hush. In the front door we went, through the living room around toward the kitchen then to the slider.

Wait. What? Chairs. Rows of chairs. Heads. Many heads. More than my family. My father came up beside me and took my arm as the three of us headed down the aisle. A real aisle. As people stood, they faced us. Aunt Sally, Ken's family and business buddies. Some people from town. A few of my clients that I had grown close to.

I felt weak in the knees when I caught site of Millie and George. Millie was already crying as George kept handing her tissues. Phyllis, of course, and some of the biking crew.

Harley!

Harley, with a tiny whisp of a woman. Well, anyone would look tiny next to Harley. But she really was just a speck.

Felix and Sofia. They had driven over from Sequim. In addition to Danny taking us through our vows, Felix prayed over us. We kissed. Ken breathed into my ear, "more." In unison Danny and Felix exclaimed, "We now pronounce you man and wife. Again!"

Everyone laughed. Then our flower girl, Felix and Sofia's granddaughter Lydia, shouted for all she was worth, "You may kiss the bride." The Miller-tants would have been proud of us. We didn't rebel; we kissed.

What I learned, mingling during our "simple" backyard reception, was that Phyliss had started calling people to share the good news. Everyone's reacted the same. They wanted to celebrate with us.

Phyllis called my mom and it snowballed from there. Millie and George, who were heading east, turned their RV around, found Whidbey on the map and started driving toward Washington.

This was supposed to be a small day, but I was lovin' how it took on a life of its own. Ken was ecstatic meeting everyone he had heard so much about. They were like old friends to him.

I would almost say, you wouldn't believe this. But you would. Harley and his mom arrived a few days early and had spent their time preparing a Cajun feast for all of us! Mom and Dad were the taste testers.

Yes, Harley's mom. It turned out she had been in a coma for quite a while laying unidentified in a long-term care facility. They didn't expect her to make it. One of her sisters found her at the facility and stayed by her side. Mom slowly recovered. Because of the hurricane, communication was spotty and records were just as bad. Try as she did, the sister could not find anything out about Harley. It was an article in the local paper that made their hearts soar. The paper was doing a series of stories title "Where are they now." Harley had been interviewed, thanks to the friend who knew he was in Washington.

I'm surprised we didn't hear their joyous halleluiahs all the way here on Whidbey when Harley was reunited with his mother. He moved her to Wenatchee where she worked right alongside of him every day while asking, almost daily, "When will you find yourself a nice woman and give me grandbabies. Our family recipes have to be passed on to the next generation. That's on you, son."

How do you let a day like that end? You don't. Most everyone stayed for a few days and we kept the party going. Now, that's the way to do a wedding.

CHAPTER SIXTY-SIX

Home Sweet

LANGLEY

At the house we did a little remodeling. This included painting inside, but we left Casey's room alone for the time being.

There we were, like anyone else. Working to keep our marriage healthy, earning a living, keeping it all balanced, being active in our church. Well, more than active. As healing wrapped our hearts, our faith became more alive than ever before. It was his love, mercy and grace that carried us through and we wanted to share that with others. We wanted to be available to people in distress or who needed an encouraging word.

Ken developed the habit of taking a run a couple of nights a]each week, something we used to do together. Even after Casey was born, we had a jogging stroller. Yet, he went alone. He'd grab his bright yellow jacket with illuminated stripes on it, kissed me on the head then leave for an hour. One night I was ready with my running sneakers on and my equally bight jacket. "Can I join you?"

Ken turned down a path we rarely used. It was rugged and ended in a dense basin of trees rather than the usual route that circled around. Tree roots disrupted our pace.

"This is my therapy." He said as we reached the end. I was jogging in place wondering what we did next. Ken threw his arms toward the treetops then open handedly began slapping his chest, a deep guttural bellow emerged sounding like a mammoth bull dying. He fell to his knees crying. I fell too, watching his face, tears welling up in my own eyes.

"Losing our sweet Casey broke me, Janine. I was shattered. But...." He turned, looked at me, wiped his wet face and took my hands. "But, losing you. Losing you."

I hadn't known Ken was aching this deeply. I knew the shop was Ken's hiding place. He crafted wood, measured, planned, sanded out the imperfections, back and forth, back and forth, rhythmically making it through each day. Then jogging at night to exercise, stay fit, but not this. This lonely place to cry out, not for Casey, but for me.

Ken tried to explain. "The first few months after we were reunited there was such relief, our love was rehabilitating. In that time the layers of grief at losing Casey had been removed. Only then did the loss of you surface."

"You have been strong for the people around you, while inside you were running a race nobody knew about. You are not alone anymore, Ken. I'm here now. I will run with you."

We did just that a few times a week. We ran. At the hollow, encircled by trees, we would fall to our knees and pray. Sometimes, yes, we still cried. We both knew that having a life again, didn't mean we never hurt, that we never missed Casey. The contradictory emotions of joy and sorrow would always be in our hearts. What we didn't want, was to hold our pain inside and have it become bitterroots. We would take the sorrow with the joy and we would do it together in the healthiest way we knew how.

CHAPTER SIXTY-SEVEN

I'm

READY

Two and a half years after losing Casey, I had half the day off. At 6:00 p.m. I heard Ken's truck come up the driveway, the engine stopped and the door opened and closed. As he entered our house with a wide grin, I knew he was bursting to tell me how the negotiations with a potential customer went. I had other news that I couldn't wait to tell him.

"I'm ready." I announced before he got underway with his story.

I was overjoyed to tell him what had flittered through my heart all day as I worked with a four-year-old recovering from a fall. Unbeknownst to his parents, he had taken his training wheels off his bike and was riding around their long driveway. A rock, out of place, challenged his riding skills and he went down hard. Through physical therapy, I was helping him regain full use of his arm that had been broken. What a sweet daredevil he was.

Yes, I was back at work, but I kept my hours to about thirty a week. For some reason, there was an urge inside of me, stirring me to try something totally new. For now, I work with kids and oh, the trouble they get into. They keep me busy enough and laughing a lot.

Ken tilted his head, his crooked smile brightening his face.

"I'm ready." I declared again.

"What. Ready? Is it dinner at your parents' house? Wait, we were there just last night. Ok tell me. I completely forgot." He was shaking his head in muddled repentance.

"I'd rather show you." I took his hand, kissed him and led him down the hallway to the second door on the right. He looked at me askance.

"Go on in." I prompted.

He opened the door and saw the pale lavender nursery. that was Casey's bedroom, changed. That afternoon I painted it in three shades of green. His favorite color.

On the wall was a shadow box with Casey's bat and the T-ball jersey she would have worn. An inscription along the bottom read, *Big Sister is Watching Over You.*

Ken took Janine's hand, "That's the jersey I got for Casey to play T-ball when we got back from Dungeness." He held my hand tighter in silence.

I broke the silence, "Remember when you were teaching her how to play, she'd do a quick skip at the plate before settling in to hit."

"Yes, and she'd cheer herself on." He looked at Janine with acknowledgement, "I'm happy for you that you were finally ready to redo this room."

"Hmmm." I said with mischievous eyes. "I'm ready." I crooked my finger imploring him to follow me.

He tilted his head, scrunched his eyebrows looking at me in confusion. "Ready?"

"To have a baby."

"Baby?

"Baby."

Ken picked me up swinging me around then abruptly put me down. I took his hand and drew him toward our bedroom.

At the bed Ken stopped abruptly, "Willie" He exclaimed. I knew he was thinking of Willie Mays.

Oh no here we go again with the baseball greats.

"What if it's a girl." Sounding very similar to a conversation we had years ago.

"Ok. Ok. A name. We need a name. Babe. Ty. Hank."

"We have time Ken. We could try tennis stars. Serena. Or golf, Tiger."

"Serene can't be a boy. Wait. I've got it. Jackie. Fits either a boy or a girl."

We tossed names at each other for months. The family joined in. Gosh there are a zillion "greats" to consider, many with names that fit either gender.

Meet Our Little One

Reggie Jacqueline Dunleavy

BORN OCTOBER 9TH AT 3:48 A.M. ~ 6 LBS 4 OZ. ~ 20"

WITH LOVE: KEN, JANINE, PEACHES AND CASEY [FROM ABOVE]

Discussion Questions

1.   Within Janine's quest to find her life we got to witness many experiences she had along the way, as well as glimpses of her past. What was the most memorable story, anecdote or example in the book? What made it stand out to you?

2.   In a crisis people tend to go into "fight" or "flight" mode. What character represents how you might respond to a crisis and why?

3.   Faith was woven into the story. How did you connect or not with this element of the book?

4.   How did getting to know Casey add to the story?

5.   We meet family and new friends as we travel with Janine. Are there characters you wish you could give advice to? What would that advice be?

6.   Janine was challenged by an inner motivation to find her life. How did the book challenge you or change your perspective or opinion on something?

7. Other than Janine, what character did you find the most intriguing or relatable or enjoyable?

8. Dungeness Spit did seem to hold a few answers for Janine. Key among them was when she and Ken decided to move forward together sharing their joys and sorrow. How did you feel about the ending?